High Seas Holiday

WeHo 2022 Holiday Edition

Sherryl D. Hancock

Published by Vulpine Press in the United Kingdom in 2022

ISBN: 978-1-83919-491-7

Cover by Claire Wood
Cover photo: Tirzah D. Hancock

www.vulpine-press.com

Happy Holidays to you and yours!
With love, from Sherryl and Tirzah

Chapter 1

"It is called what?" Remi huffed out as she lowered the weight she was hefting.

"It's called the 'Women Who Rock Our World' cruise! It's an Olivia Cruise, so all lesbians all the time," Wynter enthused.

Remi nodded. "And they want you to perform?" She sat up on the weight bench and reached for her water bottle, wincing slightly as she did.

"You're not overdoing it, are you?" Wynter's raised eyebrows told Remi what her answer better be.

Remington LaRoché, a former MMA fighter, had met the feisty rock star Wynter Kincade when she'd been appointed as Wynter's bodyguard. It had been a tumultuous assignment for the usually calm and collected fighter; at the time Wynter was having issues with her girlfriend, a petulant drug addict. What had truly bonded the singer and her bodyguard was the incident where Wynter had fallen twenty feet from an upper stage area while performing, and Remi had caught her. The world had fallen in love with the couple when cameras had caught Remi talking to Wynter, begging her not to die in her native tongue, Haitian Creole. They'd been together ever since and had been through the pandemic together. Wynter had contracted COVID from a fan in

1

China, and unfortunately, Remington had caught it from her. Remi had almost been killed by the virus. She was still working her way back to her former health and vitality.

Pressing her lips together, Remi drank from her water bottle, formulating her reply. "I have to push a little bit extra to get my strength back."

Wynter's light blue eyes narrowed as she frowned. "You almost died, babe, give yourself a bit of a break."

"I have been giving myself a break, for over a year and a half, it's time to get back."

Wynter closed her eyes for a long moment, her worry for her wife warring with her desire to understand that Remi needed her strength back for her own peace of mind. She drew in a long breath through her nose and blew it out through her mouth, trying to calm her upset. Finally, she nodded. "Okay, I get it, I'm sorry."

Remi stood from the bench and took her wife gently in her arms. "I know ti lanmou mwen, you are afraid for me, but I'm still here."

The tears caught in Wynter's throat at the endearment 'my little love.' She nestled into Remi's arms. Almost two years since Remi had nearly died, Wynter was still waking up from nightmares believing that she'd lost the love of her life. After a few minutes Wynter stepped back to wipe her eyes. Remi stayed close, gazing down at her wife.

"So they want you to perform?" Remi prompted, getting them back to a safer topic. As one of the top rock stars on the planet at that point, it would make perfect sense for the owners of the cruise line to want someone like Wynter Kincade to make an appearance on their cruises.

"Yes," Wynter confirmed, "and be on some panels too. I think they were also going to try to get ahold of Memphis and Legend."

"And this is when?"

"In mid-December; the cruise is seven days, down to Mexico."

"And BJ has okayed this?"

Wynter pressed her lips together, rolling her eyes. "They have to talk to him."

Remi simply chuckled in reply. "I wouldn't start packing just yet."

***

"The last time I approved one of my stars going somewhere at Christmas she and her group got snowed in," BJ grouched. "Tell me what this does for me?"

Tabitha rolled her eyes. "Your star wants to do it."

BJ Sparks, the owner of Badlands Records and a legendary rock star in his own right, looked at his daughter in annoyance.

"And?" BJ asked, his aquamarine eyes sparkling defiantly.

"And she and Remi deserve a vacation, and you need to give it to them," Tabitha reasoned.

BJ made a guttural noise in the back of his throat, sounding much like a growl.

"I hear Memphis and Legend are being asked as well…" Tabitha continued.

"Legend don't work for me," BJ stated simply.

3

"And you'd never tell Memphis no." Tabitha pursed her lips, her look telling her father that he was being unreasonable.

BJ's eyes narrowed dangerously. "You're telling me I'm being a prick."

"No…" Tabitha shook her head. "I'd never call you that, Daddy."

It was BJ's turn to purse his lips. "Like hell you wouldn't."

Tabitha laughed, shaking her head. "I usually call you a shithead when you're acting like this." She winked.

"You're not too old to take over my knee, ya know."

"I'll tell Mom!" Tabitha threatened with a grin.

"I'll take her over my knee too." BJ laughed.

Tabitha wrinkled her nose. "Ew, don't gross me out!"

"Fine!" BJ blew his breath out. "Go ahead and call them, but I swear," he wagged a finger at his daughter as she stood up, "if that boat sinks, you're fired!"

Tabitha laughed her way out of the office.

***

"They'd love to have you on the panel too," Legend whispered in her wife's ear.

"Mmm," Riley murmured as she snuggled back against Legend. They were spending a lazy Sunday morning in bed together. "I'd have to look at my shooting schedule. Give me the dates later, and I'll see if I can make it."

Legend Azaria was the magnetic movie director who'd captured the heart of superstar Riley Taylor. Riley had killed herself

4

to audition to play Legend's character in Legend's autobiographical film *For the Telling*. Riley ended up playing Legend's love interest Georgette. The movie had been a very intense film about being in the Marines during Don't Ask, Don't Tell. It had drawn Riley and Legend much closer, and they'd fallen in love. It wasn't a storybook romance, but it was certainly a Hollywood romance!

"It would be a nice break," Legend enticed, even as she kissed Riley's neck, her hands sliding over her wife's skin.

Riley shivered. "Okay, knock it off, you don't have to talk me into it, I just have to see what my filming schedule looks like."

Legend laughed. "I'm just making sure you understand what's at stake here."

"Uh-huh…" Riley sighed. "Alone with my wife for seven full days, along with all her adoring fans."

"As if you don't have way more fans."

"The lesbian contingent is newer," Riley told Legend. Riley had previously only dated men, and Legend had been her first and only lesbian romance.

"Oh, don't sell yourself short, I think a lot of lesbians were beyond thrilled when you came out, babe. But they've been fans for years."

Riley shook her head, smiling all the same. Legend was forever telling her that she was a lesbian darling, long before she became one.

"I guess we'll just see, won't we?"

"Only if you clear your schedule," Legend chided. "Come on, do that movie star thang."

"I'm trying to lose my bitchy reputation, thank you."

5

Legend laughed, hugging her wife close. "Yes dear."

***

"I still don't get why they want me," Memphis mumbled around a mouthful of lasagna.

"You rock their world, love," Kieran answered slyly. Her wife was known worldwide for her skills as not only a DJ, but also as a movie sound engineer.

"BJ probably won't let me do it, anyway."

"Is that a hopeful tone I hear?" Kieran chided gently. Memphis was always happiest staying behind the scenes lately, especially after her brush with COVID. Memphis had gotten sick due to an overzealous fan who'd grabbed at her in the grocery store. Since COVID seemed to be lingering, Memphis had become more reclusive, and it was worrying Kieran.

In response, Memphis only shrugged, and continued eating her lunch, but Kieran knew better. It was Kieran's feeling that Memphis needed to get back into the world, and this opportunity would give her a chance to do what she really loved, which was DJing at a club. Olivia Cruises had offered her any night at any of the clubs on board the ship.

Memphis tended to be a bit shy normally, due to a lot of childhood trauma. She'd been part of a cult that her mother had brought her into. She'd almost been the child bride to the cult's leader, but she'd escaped and lived under an assumed name for many years. During that time she'd discovered how much she loved music and had ended up attending the Art Institute and obtaining a degree in Audio Production. That had eventually parlayed into being not only a DJ, but a sound engineer for musicians, and most recently working with Legend Azaria for movie sound.

But when BJ Sparks had learned that Memphis could sing beautifully, he'd convinced her to cut a record which had garnered her many fans. Unfortunately, Memphis hadn't really wanted to be famous, so she'd never done another album. Kieran, a woman she'd met through her friend, was very understanding, but she felt that Memphis was now hiding, and it was to her detriment.

Later that afternoon, Kieran got word from Tabitha that BJ had indeed okayed Memphis going on the cruise. This news sent Memphis into a bit of a panic attack.

"He did?" Memphis squeaked.

"Yes, and I think we need to go," Kieran explained patiently.

Memphis didn't respond, she simply continued to play on the video game she'd been playing when Kieran had entered their living room. Kieran took a deep breath and sat down next to her wife. After a few minutes, she reached over and touched Memphis's hand.

"Are you processing or avoiding?" Kieran asked gently.

Memphis twitched her shoulder. "Both."

Kieran nodded. "Okay, then I will let you be so you can continue."

Kieran was cooking dinner that evening when Memphis wandered into the kitchen, turning on the Bose wireless speakers, and putting on music quietly. This told Kieran that Memphis wanted to talk. Hopping up on the counter next to where Kieran was cutting vegetables, Memphis picked up a piece of celery, took out her gum and popped the celery in her mouth.

"What would they want me to do?" Memphis asked.

Kieran continued what she was doing, knowing she needed to approach this carefully, not wanting to worry Memphis into saying no.

"I know that they want you to DJ at one of the clubs, whatever and however many nights that you want."

"Okay…" Memphis's voice told Kieran she was waiting for the other shoe to drop as she put her gum back in her mouth.

"They asked that you be on one of the panels."

"Meaning."

"Meaning that you'd be asked questions by members of the audience."

Memphis's lips twitched. "Is that a requirement?"

Kieran hesitated, sensing that this was a pivotal question. "I don't think it's required, but I think it would be good thing for you to do."

"Why?" Memphis countered, shrugging. "What do I have to say that people want to hear?"

Kieran put down her knife and looked up at her wife. "I think people want to hear how someone who came from such difficult beginnings made it through her life to become what you are today."

"A DJ," Memphis stated flatly.

"A DJ, a sound engineer, a brilliant artist."

8

"No." Memphis started shaking her head. "Not that artist part, no."

"You don't have to talk about that part," Kieran reasoned, "but it is part of who you are, lovey, like it or not."

Memphis had done one album, singing her own songs, and people had loved it. Unfortunately, the insecure, very private person that Memphis was made it difficult for her to even consider touring to support the album, and she'd flat out refused to do another album.

Memphis blew her breath out, doing her best to calm the mild panic attack that was threatening to bloom. "I just can't, Kier, I can't talk about that."

"You don't have to, love."

"But what if someone asks?"

"Then you tell them you don't intend to do another album. Simple as that."

Memphis chewed on her gum, as she considered what her wife had just said. "Simple as that," she repeated, not sounding fully convinced. "And I get to DJ."

"Yes."

"As many times as I want?"

"Yes."

More chewing ensued. "And do the panel?"

"Yes."

"And that's it?"

"Yes."

Memphis drew in a deep breath, blowing it out slowly. "Okay, I'll do it."

"Ace," Kieran replied, smiling brightly.

***

"We could do a side trip to El Quelite…" Raine commented.

Natalia turned around, having been working on a new dance routine in their living room. Her eyes lit up at the mention of the town she was from, but then she frowned. "Can we even afford it? Those cruises must be expensive."

"I checked into it," Raine told her, "we can make payments, like $70 a month."

"We can definitely do that…" Natalia nodded excitedly, grabbing Raine's arm. "I can finally introduce you to my family."

"And we can finally set a wedding date." Raine winked.

"Mocosa!" Natalia gasped, calling her fiancée a brat in Spanish. "You know that's not why."

"Well, we needed to save up money, too, to do it right."

"Exactly!"

"But meeting your family was important too," Raine put in.

"It was…it is," Natalia corrected.

"Did you want to get married down there?"

Once again, Natalia's eyes lit up. "You'd really do that?"

"If it would make you happy, I would do anything."

In truth, Raine had no family to invite to their wedding; her mother had abandoned her when she was five and she'd never known her father. She'd been a product of the foster care system, which she'd opted out of when she was fifteen, instead choosing to make it on her own. Making it on her own had included getting

10

into the The Juilliard School in New York on a full scholarship. But she'd left that world when her best friend had died right after they graduated.

She'd come to Los Angeles and had gotten into law enforcement. That had made her a new circle of friends, including a beautiful cardio dance teacher, Natalia. Raine had been drawn to Natalia for her talent, and because she'd become a caring compassionate friend right away.

"I think it's a wonderful idea!" Natalia said, hoping against hope that her family would love Raine the way that she did.

Raine nodded. "Then we'll say yes to the cruise."

"I wonder who else is going?" Natalia mused.

***

"Is it safe at this point?" McKenna worried.

Cody shrugged. "They're doing cruises again, so I'm guessing it must be."

"I've heard Norovirus is rampant on those things," Jazmine commented.

"Don't say that!" Dakota warned. "Now they'll never say yes."

The four were having breakfast together. Dakota had come over to help Cody finish a couple of things at her and McKenna's home. Things they'd started during the Coronavirus outbreak but hadn't finished due to Cody going back to doing undercover work.

As a contractor, Dakota was always working on home projects, and not finishing something she'd started drove her crazy.

11

"Who all is going?" Cody asked.

"I know Nat and Raine are," Jazmine put in.

"Wynter and Remi, Legend, and hopefully Riley, even Memphis is foraying out of her cave to go." Dakota added the last as a challenge.

"Hey," Cody narrowed her eyes, "I've been out there, it sucks."

"Yeah, yeah." Dakota rolled her eyes. "Just come, it'll be fun."

McKenna looked over at her wife, reaching out to take her hand. "You could definitely use a break, babe."

"We both could," Cody agreed.

Cody had been working almost non-stop since the pandemic had let up, and it was starting to wear on her. McKenna had been busy as well; as a board-certified psychiatrist she worked with Cody's mother in a children's home. So many children had been displaced during the pandemic. They seemed to pour into the home, and it certainly kept McKenna busy. She and Cody felt like they never saw each other.

"Yeah, weren't you two supposed to be working on having a kid or something?" Dakota commented with a wry grin.

Jazmine shook her head, looking heavenward. "My wife, the queen of subtlety."

Dakota simply laughed, shrugging. "The longer it takes them to have a kid, the more time our moms have to wonder why we're not having any."

"Yeah, what's up with that?" Cody raised an eyebrow.

"We're not having kids," Dakota stated emphatically.

McKenna canted her head. "Can I ask why?"

Dakota looked over at Jazmine, silently asking if she wanted to answer. They'd had a long discussion about this topic the year before, they'd just never really said anything to anyone else.

"We just don't think it's our thing," Jazmine told them. "I've never really wanted kids, and while Dak loves kids…"

"I don't want any of our own either," Dakota finished, not wanting their friends to believe that it was just Jazmine's decision. "It was a mutual decision."

Cody and McKenna exchanged a look of surprise, but both nodded, accepting what they were being told.

"Have you told the moms?" Cody asked.

Cody and Dakota were the adopted children of Savanna and Lyric Falco. Both Cody and Dakota had rough beginnings in their lives, having been on their own from an early age and becoming friends on the street. Cody had been arrested for stealing, but had gotten lucky and been put into a children's home with Savanna. That had been where she'd met the women that would become her mothers. Cody had gone a separate path, but had ended up back in Los Angeles, and through some rough times of her own, had ended up winning the hearts of Savanna and Lyric. Dakota had been adopted as an adult, but she loved their family all the same.

"It really hasn't come up," Dakota commented mildly, her eyes narrowing slightly. "But I'm betting it will now, won't it?"

Cody grinned mischievously.

"Oh you!" McKenna swatted her wife on the arm. "Let them tell your mothers in their own time. What is wrong with you?"

13

"So many things…" Cody sighed. "But this might keep them off our backs for a bit."

"You've been married longer than us!" Dakota exclaimed.

"So? You're hiding stuff from them!" Cody retorted.

"No, I just haven't talked to them about it."

Cody smiled. "No time like dinner tomorrow night."

"I swear, you two…" Jazmine shook her head.

"She started it!" Dakota accused.

"Look who's whining." Cody made a face.

"You did start it," Dakota snapped, sticking her tongue out at Cody.

Jazmine and McKenna merely shook their heads.

"Why have kids?" Jazmine commented to McKenna, gesturing to Cody and Dakota.

"Kind of redundant," McKenna agreed.

"Hey…" Cody gave her wife a narrowed look, only to have it spoiled by her grin. "So, cruise? Yes?"

"I say yes," McKenna commented.

"Yep," Dakota chimed in.

"Definitely," Jazmine happily agreed.

***

"What's this about no kids?" Savanna commented at diner the following night.

Cody snickered, even as Dakota threw her a dirty look. Looking at her mother, Dakota shrugged. "Just not our thing."

Lyric nodded. "I get that."

Savanna raised an eyebrow. "You do?"

"Sure," Lyric said with a flip of her hand. "I never wanted kids either."

"Uh…" Cody stammered, even as Anastasia, Lyric and Savanna's six-year-old daughter, came bounding into the room. Cody gestured to the child as she picked her up in a bear hug.

"Your mom changed my mind." Lyric winked at Savanna.

"Well, nobody is changing anybody's mind here." Dakota held up her hands in defense.

"Relax, babe, I don't think they're trying," Jazmine told her wife.

"Nope." Savanna shook her head. "Whether or not to have kids is up to you, I was just hoping for more babies, and your mom's told me no, so…"

"So it's up to us," Cody told McKenna. "That's where that 'so' was going." She winked at her wife.

"I gathered that one." McKenna grinned. "We are going to start trying again here soon. I just wanted to wait till things were more stable with the virus."

Savanna sighed. "I think it's as stable as it's going to get."

"Yeah, I think it's going to end up being like the flu shot we get every year," Lyric agreed, as she brought rolls to the table. "How's your case going, Code?"

Cody sighed, grabbing a roll and taking a bite. "A lot slower than I'd like, but I think I'm finally getting some traction in this new place."

Savanna shuddered, shaking her head. She still didn't like that their daughter frequently put herself in danger to catch human

15

traffickers. Cody was an undercover officer that posed as an underage runaway to try and bring down corruption in children's homes. Because of her young looks, Cody blended in quite well with other homeless teens.

Lyric caught her wife's gesture, and pointedly changed the subject. "What's your latest project, Dak?"

"Working on this huge Victorian over in Burbank, four bed, five bath, big monstrosity."

"Wow, who needs more bathrooms than they do bedrooms?" McKenna asked.

"Guest bathrooms?" Cody shrugged.

"Oh, this thing's a mess!" Dakota enthused. "I'm ripping out walls, patching plumbing, all kinds of crazy crap!"

"Crap!" Anastasia happily repeated.

"Dak…" Lyric warned.

"What?" Dakota replied. "It's not the S-word or anything."

"What's the S-word?" Anastasia immediately queried.

"Stupid," Cody commented, winking at her adopted sister.

"Silly," Jazmine added.

"Strange." McKenna laughed.

"Stupendous!" Savanna called from the kitchen.

"Stifling," Dakota muttered.

"Shutting up," Lyric finished, and the group laughed.

Later during dinner, they discussed the cruise the girls had decided to go on.

"So it's down to Mexico?" Savanna asked.

"Yeah, like Mazatlán, Puerto Vallarta," Dakota told her.

"Cabo San Lucas," Cody chimed in.

"Who came up with this idea?" Lyric asked.

"Well, it started with Wynter," Dakota told them. "She got invited by the cruise line for their 'Women Who Rock Our World' cruise."

"Well, there you go." Lyric smiled.

"It's an Olivia Cruise," McKenna told them.

"A what?" Savanna asked.

"They're lesbo cruises." Dakota chuckled. "I mean, lesbian cruises," she corrected when she saw her younger sister perk up.

"Oh, wow, that's nice." Lyric smiled. "About time we have our own thing."

"So Wynter is performing?" Savanna clarified.

"Yep, and she's on the panel for a question-and-answer session. Legend and maybe Riley will be there and so will Memphis," Cody told them.

"Sounds like it'll be a fun trip."

"You guys could come," Jazmine offered.

"Oh, no." Lyric shook her head. "No ships for me thanks."

"Seasick?" McKenna queried sympathetically.

"And then some!" Lyric nodded, with a grin. "When is it?"

"Right before Christmas," Cody said.

"You'll be back for Christmas, though, right?" Savanna asked.

Dakota rolled her eyes. "Yes, Mom, we'll be back."

"You better be," Savanna muttered.

***

17

"They want us to do what again?" Gray asked from the bedroom closet.

Rayden moved to stand in the doorway to their walk-in closet, the closet that her wife was in the middle of reorganizing. "If you'd get your head out from under the clothes, you might be able to hear me."

Gray shuffled out from under the hanging jackets she was attempting to untangle from each other's hangers, her blonde hair tousled from the project, making her wife smile. Rayden pulled the enmeshed hangers from the closet rod and fixed them, before putting them back.

"That's easy for you because you're way tall," Gray commented.

"You could ask me for help."

"I could, but then you'd be in my way." Gray smiled cheekily up at her wife.

Rayden never got over how beautiful Gray was, and she was grateful on a daily basis she still had her. A few years earlier, when Gray was still a pilot for the Air Force, she'd gone down with her plane, and was thought to be dead. Rayden had been lost, so much so she'd left their home in Washington D.C. to take a job in California working for Jericho Tehrani at the Department of Justice. When Grayson reappeared, Rayden had been shocked, but she'd also been determined to forever show Gray every day how much she loved her.

"Uh-huh," Rayden murmured, as she moved back to the doorway of the closet. "Anyway, Cody was telling me about this cruise they're going on in December."

"In December? Won't it be cold?" Gray interrupted.

"It's a holiday kind of thing." Rayden waved away the question. "Wynter is performing, Remi, Legend, Nat and Raine are going…they invited us to go too."

"A cruise?" Gray repeated.

"Yes, darling, a cruise," Rayden reiterated patiently.

"To where? 'Cause I'm not going to Alaska!"

Rayden chuckled. "I don't think they do cruises to Alaska in the winter, dear. It's to Mexico."

"Oh," Gray said simply, then shrugged. "Okay."

"That easy, huh?" Rayden mused.

Gray walked over to Rayden, putting her arms up around her wife's neck. "I know you, you've researched it, figured out the cost, checked if we could afford it, verified the weather patterns, checked the tidal schedule, double-checked the crime rate in the ports of call…"

Rayden was laughing halfway into her litany. "Okay, okay, I'm not that ridiculous."

Gray smiled. "You're a planner, babe, it's okay, one of us has to be."

Rayden glanced at the closet behind her wife. "And you're the—"

"Organizer!" Gray supplied before her wife could come up with another noun.

Rayden nodded, licking her lips. "For now."

"Oh, stop, I'll finish this, I promise."

An hour later, Rayden walked into their bedroom and saw a number of odd items on their bed.

"And what is this?" she called, picking up a single shoe that had no mate.

Gray walked into the room surveying the small pile on the bed. "Those are the misfits."

"The misfits?" Rayden repeated.

"Yeah, the things that don't go with anything else."

"Okay…and you're going to do what with them?" Rayden asked.

Gray looked back at the pile for a long moment, then bit her lip looking up at her wife. "Put them in a box in case their friends turn up?"

Rayden shook her head. "No."

"Put them in a corner of the room until they crawl off to find their matches?"

"No," Rayden said again.

"Put them at the top of the closet until you forget about them?"

"Gray…"

"I know, I know, I need to get rid of them, but as soon as I do, they're sole mate will show up!"

"Sole as in s-o-l-e?" Rayden raised an eyebrow.

"It works for both shoes and socks." Gray laughed.

Rayden just shook her head. "Please just throw them out."

"But…"

"No."

"But I could—"

"No."

"But let me just—"

"Gray…"

"Ray…"

Rayden sighed. "You drive me crazy, woman."

"I know, but you love me." Gray smiled.

The pile was moved to the closet and unbeknownst to Gray, shoes disappeared one by one, never to be seen again. It was how their marriage worked.

***

"It wouldn't hurt for you to go," Gage commented to Harley in their one-on-one meeting that week.

Harley sighed. "That's what Shi is telling me, too."

"Well, she's right, we'll be in what's hopefully going to be our quiet season, so less computer drama to worry about."

"But we wanted to work on that cut over to the new server then."

"Harley, you can do that at any point during the winter." Harley's lips twitched; Shiloh had said much the same thing. "Get out, get some fresh air, have an adventure."

Harley blew her breath out in a rush. "Fine! I feel like everyone's trying to get rid of me."

"No, we're trying to help you go have some fun."

"Their Wi-Fi will likely suck," Harley grumbled, which only made Gage laugh.

"So Gage actually wants you to go?" Shiloh asked later that morning.

Harley shrugged. "Pretty much."

21

"Boy, rough gig." Shiloh rolled her eyes. "Your boss encouraging to go take a vacation."

Harley narrowed her eyes at her girlfriend. "You know, sarcasm hurts, Shi."

"Blah, blah, blah," Shiloh muttered, winking at Harley.

As one of the best computer programmers around, Harley Marie Davidson was highly sought after, not that you'd ever know it by her lack of ego about her skills. Harley was one of the most down to earth people one could ever meet. She also had ADHD to the enth power, so that tended to make her appear out of it or spacey. In truth, she tended to hyper-focus on projects to the point of blocking everything and anyone out. Shiloh was her constant aid and companion, always helping her navigate being social, while still staying on track with projects, but not to the detriment of her health. It was also Shiloh's self-appointed job to block anyone who would see fit to harm Harley, emotionally or mentally.

Harley had been appointed as Deputy Chief of IT Services at the California Office of Emergency Services. As such there were often Bureau Chiefs who felt they could attempt to force their issues onto Harley and do their best to make their project a priority. Quite often anyone that had previously been nasty or overly pushy with Harley didn't get past Shiloh's desk outside Harley's office. It was also well known that Shiloh had a direct line to Gage, the Director of OES, and Shiloh would not hesitate to use that power if anyone, regardless of rank, harassed Harley.

Their relationship was very symbiotic, everyone knew that Shiloh was Harley's protector and biggest fan at the same time.

Shiloh understood the sometimes-eccentric programmer like no one ever had, and all of Harley's friends loved her for that. Harley loved Shiloh, craving the safety and sanity that Shiloh brought into her life. She did her very best to show Shiloh how much she loved her, more than she'd ever done with any other partner in her life. Harley recognized that Shiloh was her balance in life, so she did her best to set aside some of her more annoying habits, and be present when her partner was around.

"So, I'm clearing your calendar for December 8 through December 19," Shiloh stated as she sat in front of Harley's desk on her cell phone.

"How long is that cruise?" Harley asked, horrified.

Shiloh grinned. "It's only seven days, but that leaves us time to pack and unpack when we get home. Breathe, babe. It's just a vacation. You can bring your laptop, and I'll even let you use it an hour each day." She said the last with a wink, drawing a scowl from Harley, which only made her chuckle.

"There better be good drinks," Harley muttered darkly.

Chapter 2

February 20, 2022

"Holy shit, how much?" Cody exclaimed.

"I warned you that artificial insemination wasn't going to be cheap," McKenna told her wife.

"But that much?"

"Well, we could try doing ourselves at home…" McKenna commented.

Cody gave her a deadpan look. "Have you never seen *If These Walls Could Talk 2*? Hell no."

McKenna raised an eyebrow. "No, I haven't, what's that?"

Cody gave her a shocked look, but then remembered that McKenna hadn't been a lesbian before they'd met. "Okay, it's all about lesbian relationships through the years. And there's one story that centers around two lesbians trying to get pregnant. It's funny as hell, it's Ellen DeGeneres and Sharon Stone are the couple, and when it's time to do the insemination, Ellen is the one to go get the sperm, and Sharon is the one that stays home to get everything ready. Oh my God the funniest part is when Ellen is home with the sperm and Sharon has boiled the turkey baster they are planning to use for the insemination, and it's all curled up from the heat… Ellen says 'Are you trying to make things difficult?' It is so damned, funny…but yeah babe, that would happen to us."

"So, I'm guessing no for the home insemination," McKenna surmised.

"Right you are."

"Then yeah, it's going to be expensive."

Cody curled her lips up in annoyance, but nodded. "I guess it costs what it costs."

"Maybe we'll get lucky like Savanna did," McKenna offered. "Didn't she get pregnant that first time?"

"With my uncle's sperm, maybe we should ask him to donate. Ana turned out alright."

"Alright?" McKenna gasped. "She's gorgeous. Do you think he'd do it?"

Cody shrugged. "I don't know why not, he's never having any of his own."

"He can't stay with one woman long enough to do that," McKenna murmured.

Cody smiled. "Yeah, he is kind of a whore."

McKenna narrowed her eyes. "It runs in the family."

Cody opened her mouth to protest, but then just grinned, because she knew her wife was right, she had been a bit of a whore before she'd met McKenna.

"I'll ask him, he might be getting up there, but I'm sure he's still got it." Cody winked lasciviously.

"That'll save us money."

"How much?" Cody asked quizzically.

"About fifteen hundred dollars."

"Sperm costs fifteen hundred dollars?" Cody looked skeptical. "These guys jack off for free constantly."

McKenna made a face. "Don't gross me out, please?"

Cody smirked. "You were married to one of those."

"Bleh," McKenna stuck out her tongue, "don't remind me! This is way closer to sperm than I ever wanted to have to get again."

Cody couldn't help but laugh. "I hear ya, babe, I hear ya."

"And I probably saved us money by listening to your mom about taking my basal temperature and clocking my periods. So we're way ahead of the game. We'd just have to get a doctor that will work with us on the insemination part."

"Well, that's something. Didn't Finley say she knew someone?"

"She did, I'll call her tomorrow."

***

"My family is so excited to see us!" Natalia informed Raine.

She'd been trying to get ahold of her family for a month; she'd wanted them all together when she told them she was coming down, and bringing Raine.

Raine smiled, happy that Natalia's family sounded like they were okay with meeting her, though it didn't make her any less nervous about the whole thing. She knew that Natalia's family was very tight knit, and that her family had not been happy about Natalia coming to America to study, and not coming home even

26

when she'd gotten her degree the year before. Raine also knew that part of the reason Natalia hadn't gone home to her family was their relationship. It was a concern that Natalia's family would hold that against the newcomer. She also knew that Natalia's family being excited to see 'them' didn't necessarily extend to her, just maybe they were excited to see Natalia at all. It had been years since she'd been home. Four years to be exact.

"That's good," Raine encouraged.

Natalia tilted her head. "Aye mija, you still think they don't like you?"

Raine set her bag down as she tried to figure out how to answer. "I think that they know you haven't been home because of me."

"I haven't been home because of things like school and COVID," Natalia responded vehemently.

"And me."

"Aye si, maybe a little bit you too," Natalia begrudgingly answered.

"A little?"

"Muy poca," Natalia responded darkly, saying very little.

Raine laughed, nodding. "Si amor, muy poca. But trust me, they know."

"They are happy for me!"

"That doesn't mean that they aren't unhappy with me," Raine reasoned.

"Well," Natalia began, her hands squarely on her hips, "we will just have to see who is right this time, mocosa."

"Yes, mocosa mas grande," Raine answered, calling Natalia a bigger brat. Natalia's mouth opened in mock offense, then she picked up a tissue box nearby and threw it at Raine, missing her by a foot. "Still gotta work on your throwing arm."

"Aye dios mio," Natalia began, rattling off a few more obscenities making Raine roar with laughter. The matter was forgotten soon after.

***

Riley's long blonde hair blew in the breeze, her blue eyes shining in the sunlight. Gazing up at Trent, she sighed deeply. "There will never be another man like you."

"But there'll be other men," Trent replied darkly.

Riley looked sad for a moment, then a slow smile began on her face. "But they won't be you." Raising the pistol, she fired one shot, straight into his forehead. The surprised look on Trent's face just before he fell off the cliff, made Riley smile even wider, her eyes sparkling with the malice that she finally allowed to show. It was over.

"Cut!" the director yelled, his glee evident in the tenor of his voice.

Trent stood up from the air cushion he'd fallen on. They'd CGI in the cliff during editing. Climbing off the cushion, he walked over to Riley, who was taken a long drink of her iced tea. He touched her on the back, smiling down at her.

"That was fantastic!"

Riley turned, so his hand fell away from her as she glanced up at him. She nodded. "It was good. Hopefully this is the last time we'll have to do it." They'd done the scene four times already.

"I don't mind, getting to work with the infamous Riley Taylor is such a rush," Trent enthused.

Riley quirked her lips slightly with a fake smile. She noticed he was standing a bit closer suddenly, so she stepped back. Lifting her head to look up at him, she faked another smile. "That's nice of you to say."

"Nice?" he replied, a slick smile flashing bright white teeth creased his face. "That's all?" This time there was a definite come on to the tone of his voice.

Riley pressed her lips together, having dealt with his kind her entire career. It was all about stroking their ego, while they pretended to stroke hers. She'd never really realized how disgusted she was by all of it until the last few years. It was exhausting playing these little games, and while she really wanted to ball up her fist and punch him in his perfectly capped teeth, she also didn't want to become a pariah in the industry. Women who pummeled their co-stars usually had trouble finding work after that.

Searching for something to respond with that didn't sound bitchy, Riley settled for a small laugh and then she made a point of drifting away from him. Fortunately, it was their last scene for the day so she went to her trailer to take off her makeup and change clothes.

Later, as she was coming out of her trailer, she noted that Trent was lounging just outside, waiting for her. Jesus, she thought to herself, the guy just doesn't take a hint!

"I thought I'd walk you to your car," he offered as if she should be honored.

Trent Harrison was discovered later in life, at the age of thirty, and had been starring in movies for the past five years. It was well known that he'd been making up for lost time sleeping with every famous actress he could get with in order to establish himself as a player on the Hollywood scene. This wasn't the first time he'd come on to Riley during filming, but she'd manage to cajole and joke her way out of offending him every time. As filming was wrapping up, however, he was seemingly becoming more desperate, and it was starting to become a problem.

"I didn't drive," Riley began, even as she walked past him toward the parking lot.

"Oh, well, no problem! I can take you anywhere you want to go." Trent beamed, his tone somewhat leering as he fell into step beside her.

Riley lengthened her strides to try to get ahead of him, not wanting him to be breathing down her neck. Unfortunately, Trent's strides were a lot longer than hers, so he kept up easily.

"I don't think you understand," Riley tried to tell him as they rounded the corner of the sound stage.

"No, I don't think you understand." Trent smiled looking highly predatory. "I really want this to happen." He put his arm around Riley's shoulders as they walked.

"What do you want to happen?" Riley asked, stopping in her tracks, shrugging off his arm.

Trent had the temerity to look confused for a moment. "This," he said, gesturing between the two of them. "You, me."

Riley canted her head. "You do realize I'm married, right?"

Once again, Trent looked befuddled. "Well, yeah, but…" His voice trailed off as he held up a hand dismissively.

Riley shook her head, and continued to walk, seeing her ride waiting for her. Trent hurried to catch up.

"Hey." Riley smiled at her wife, who was waiting for her, leaning against her cherry red 1970 Barracuda. Legend was dressed in all black, including combat boots. The only thing that caught the street lights that were just coming on was the silver chain that dipped from her pocket.

Trent noted the nasty set to the woman's lips, as well as the glare Legend was sending his way. Legend pushed off the car, striding toward them with such intensity that Trent found himself backing up a couple of steps. However, the well-known director merely reached out to take her wife's bag from her, and leaned in to kiss Riley's lips. She swung the bag over her shoulder, and directed another look toward Trent, her eyes dark points of fire.

"You touch my wife again without her permission, it'll be the last time, I assure you," Legend told him, taking Riley's hand and starting to walk her to the car.

Trent was foolish enough to snicker, feeling self-assured with his size and the fight training he'd been taking, thinking he could handle the smaller woman. "What're you gonna do?"

Legend stopped, dropping Riley's hand as she turned around, a sneer on her lips. "You're an actor, right?"

Trent was surprised by the question, and huffed out a laugh. "Well, yeah."

"Wanna continue to be one?" Legend queried, as she canted her head slightly.

"What are you talking about?" Trent snapped, thinking this woman was actually stupid enough to threaten his life.

"I'm talking about your burgeoning career," Legend specified. Trent threw up both his hands, still not getting it. "Have you ever heard the term blacklisting?"

This time Trent's mouth dropped open, but then he shook his head. "You don't have that kind of power."

Legend's look changed to one of amusement. "Wanna bet?"

Trent stared back at the dark-eyed director. Of course, he knew who she was, Legend Azaria was very well known in Hollywood. She was well known for being very intense about her work, and was given to fits of rage when things didn't go as she wanted or expected. The director every starlet wanted to work with, she was also known for bedding her starlets quite frequently. It was for that reason that he figured Riley would sleep with him. Obviously lesbians weren't faithful. Hell, Riley had always been with men, so she was probably only with Legend for the money.

"I'm a star!" Trent scoffed. "You can't blacklist me!"

"Dude." Legend shook her head, looking supremely confident. "I can end you with a phone call."

"Bullshit," Trent blustered.

"Wanna try me?" Legend's crooked grin lit her eyes with malevolence. "Boy, let me make things easy for you. Keep your fucking hands to yourself. Touch what's mine again, and I'll make you wish you'd never come to this town. I know people that don't play by the rules, and can make you disappear. You'll be a faint memory of that guy that was in movies once." She canted her head. "We clear?"

Trent swallowed convulsively a few times, not really ready to test Legend's reach. Finally, he nodded, turned, and walked back the way he came.

Legend smiled as she turned around to take her wife's hand again. "Simple as that."

"Would you really blacklist him?" Riley asked on the way home.

A slow smile spread across Legend's face. "In a heartbeat."

***

Jazmine stared at Dakota for a full minute, scanning her from head to toe, her look a mix between horror and humor.

"What happened to you?" Jazmine asked trying to keep from laughing.

Dakota was covered in paint. She'd wiped most of it from her face and arms, but her hair was covered, as were her clothes and work boots. Worst of all it was a lovely shade of peach.

"Remember that kid Ski I hired?" Dakota asked, her voice shaking somewhat. "You know, the one you said, 'oh give her a chance!'" Her voice raised an octave, making Jazmine cringe.

"So…not good," Jazmine surmised.

"No, Jaz…no, not good! The frigging kid just caused a chain reaction where I ended up covered in paint!"

"How?" Jazmine had the temerity to ask.

Dakota sighed loudly as she made her way into the bathroom, sitting down on the toilet to begin unlacing her work boots with angry yanks. "First it was her carrying a roll of carpet up the stairs, something she's not strong enough to do, by the way…The roll started to slip, so instead of carefully setting it down, not this kid, no…she tries to be tough and hitches it up on her shoulder, which makes her bobble the whole roll…It fell, over the railing of the stairs, down onto the ladder the guy hanging the chandelier is on. He falls, landing thankfully on the carpet roll, but that set the rest of the carpet rolling out. The unfurling carpet smacks the painter's ladder, who is painting just above my damned head as I walk out into the foyer. Guess where the can of Pleasing Peach, that was custom ordered by the way, ended up?"

Jazmine grimaced, gesturing to Dakota as a whole. "Pleasing Peach?"

"Yes, Jaz, Pleasing fucking Peach!" Dakota snapped as she started to unbutton her jeans. Jazmine put her hand to her mouth, doing her very best not to burst into laughter. Dakota held up a warning finger. "Don't you dare…"

Jazmine lost it when she saw that there was a glob of Pleasing Peach on the finger Dakota was warning her with; it had come off her jean buttons. As Jaz was consumed with howling laughter, Dakota looked at her finger, then walked toward her girlfriend and proceeded to wipe the paint in her cheek. The fight was on. They ended up wrestling all around the bedroom, Dakota getting as much paint on her girl as possible. They ended up on the bed, proceeding to fall on the floor, and both of them breaking into gales of laughter.

They "made up" in the shower for the next hour, only getting out when they realized how much water they were wasting.

"This is where a tankless water heater is a problem," Dakota commented as they dried off. "Usually, you're cued to stop when the water runs cold."

Jazmine smiled. "Well, we were a little busy…" She trailed a painted nail down Dakota's bicep.

"Uh-huh." Dakota chuckled. "Now, I'm hungry. Let's grab dinner out."

"Okay, but I have a class at seven."

"That works, I was hoping to get in a workout tonight anyway. Remi is going to be running a class tonight too," Dakota said as she pulled workout clothes out of her dresser.

"Great! I'm glad to hear she's getting back to it."

***

"I'm dyin'!" Quinn complained.

"She's trying to kill us," Rayden commented.

"She wasn't mean before COVID," Dakota grunted.

"She was definitely mean before COVID, I assure you," Kai told them.

The four were straining to hold themselves at half a pull-up. Their bodies were trembling with the effort.

"Anlé!" Remi called. "Up!" she repeated in English.

"We're expected to speak Creole now too?" Dakota asked.

"You understood it, dint you?" Quinn growled.

Dakota grunted with effort. "Yeah, yeah."

35

"Dasann! Down!" Remi called. "Learning Creole is just a bonus." She winked at Dakota as she walked by. "And I wasn't mean, zanmi mwen," she told Kai, calling her 'my friend.' "I was tough because you needed it."

Kai sighed. "I know, enstab."

"En-what?" Rayden asked, as they pulled up once again.

"Unstoppable," Kai told her.

"Pay attention!" Remi snapped. "Up!"

It was a grueling hour and afterwards the four lay on the mats breathing heavily. "I don't think I can get up," Dakota commented.

"I don't think I can move," Rayden said.

"I'm dead," Quinn replied.

"Yer not dead, till I say so," Kai told Quinn, laughing.

"Why did I think this was a good idea tonight?" Dakota moaned. "I'm not gonna be able to get up for work tomorrow."

Wynter walked into the workout room, having just finished Jazmine's dance class. She surveyed the mat and chuckled.

"You broke them," she commented to her wife.

"I made them work," Remi replied calmly, but she had a twinkle of mischief in her eyes.

"You wanted to kill them," Wynter chided.

"I wanted them to get back to proper workouts."

"Proper, meaning yours," Wynter observed.

Remi grinned. "I might have pushed a little harder than necessary."

Wynter sighed. "If you break all of our friends, who are we going to hang out with?"

Remi laughed.

Quinn was the first up, she walked over and shook Remi's hand with a big smile. "Good to have you back."

Rayden finally made it up off the floor. She patted Remi on the back. "Always good to get the blood flowing again."

"Wi wé?"

"Huh?" Rayden queried.

"Yes, see?" Remi repeated. "Apologies, my friend. I'm pleased you're still up to it."

"The only easy day was yesterday," Rayden commented, using a well-known Navy Seal saying. It was the way most Navy Seals stayed motivated.

"Oorah," Remi replied with a nod.

Kai walked over next, shaking Remi's hand. "Good to be training with you again, my friend." It had been Kai Temple who'd trained Remi for many of her fights in the past.

"Bon pou tounen, good to be back." Remi nodded smiling.

Dakota walked up last, looking a little worse for the wear. "I'm probably going to die later, so…" she said, letting her voice trail off as she grinned.

"Take a good soak, and some Motrin before bed, and lots of water until then." Remi laughed, seeing the doubtful look on Dakota's face. "It works, my friend. Try it!"

"I'll try, but if I fall asleep in the tub and drown, Jaz is gonna be mad at you."

Remi laughed, shaking her head. After everyone left, Wynter help Remi clean up and sanitize the equipment.

"You're happy to be back," Wynter observed.

"Absoliman," Remi replied with a nod of her head.

Wynter knew it had been rough on Remington not training anyone. Their lives were finally getting back on track, and for that Wynter would always be grateful.

On their drive home, Wynter looked over at her wife. "I heard from Jazmine that Cody and McKenna are trying to start having a baby."

"Vreman?" Remi looked surprised.

"Yes, really." Wynter chuckled, she never knew if Remi realized how often she used her native language. Remi had spent a lot of time teaching Wynter Haitian Creole, and Wynter was actually getting fairly good at understanding her wife. "I guess they are going to talk to Lyric's brother about donating so they can have a baby that's more like Lyric's family."

Remi nodded. "I suppose that makes some kind of sense."

"It saves them money too, the process can be pretty expensive."

Remi nodded again, but didn't comment. Wynter looked over at the woman she loved more than life. "Have you ever thought about it?"

"Sou kisa?" Remi sounded distracted.

"About what…" Wynter repeated. "About having kids, Remi."

Remi's look was shocked as she glanced over at Wynter. "Not really, no." Then she drew in a deep breath. "Was it something you wanted?"

Wynter hesitated, thinking about her answer, not wanting to say something off the cuff, knowing her wife took things very seriously when she said them. "I didn't before, you know when I was with Lauren…"

"Because that would have been redundant," Remi put in.

Wynter chuckled, her ex-girlfriend had indeed acted like a spoiled child a number of times in their relationship. It was when she'd become an abusive spoiled child that it had become a real problem.

"But the idea of having a child with you, that's a whole other thought."

Remington nodded slowly. "Are you saying it's something you want to think about doing?"

"Is it something you'd want?"

Remi was quiet for a long moment. "I would be honored to have a child with you."

Remington was from a family of horse breeders, who lived in Kentucky, and her father had taught her how to be the perfect gentleman. It was something that had attracted Wynter to her. Remi believed in not speaking ill of other people, not spreading rumors, standing when a woman entered a room, all things that made her so very different from Lauren.

Wynter felt a warm feeling flow through her. She knew she was married to the most wonderful woman she could have ever found. Reaching over, she took Remi's hand, squeezing it gently. "Let's talk about it some more, okay?"

"As you wish, mon amour."

Harley turned over in bed, rubbing her eyes. She reached down to grab her extra pillow from the floor and put it over her head. Turning over, she held the pillow down harder. Frustrated, she threw the pillow across the room with a grunt and turned over again.

"Harl?" Shiloh murmured tiredly. "What is going on?"

"Bird," Harley muttered.

"What?"

"Bird, damned bird," Harley grumbled.

Shiloh listened for a minute and could hear a bird chirping somewhere outside their window. "It's not that loud…"

"Loud enough for me to fixate on," Harley bemoaned. "Every time the damned thing chirps I can see it."

"See it?" Shiloh queried, not sure she'd just heard correctly.

"Yeah," Harley said, canting her head. "I guess normal people don't see sound, huh?"

"Well, I don't know about 'normal' but I know I don't. What does it look like?" Shiloh was always curious about the way Harley's mind worked.

"Kind of like drops in a calm pool, I get like waves from the sound, in my head."

"Whoa, that's wild, no wonder it drives you crazy."

"Yep." Harley curled her lips in dismay. "And his waves like bright red."

"Oh babe," Shiloh sympathized. Because Harley had ADHD she had a hard time with random sounds. Her mind would focus on the sound, and when she was trying to do something like sleep, it made it impossible to do. Now hearing that she could 'see' things with the sound just made Shiloh feel even more sympathetic to her girlfriend's plight. "What can I do?"

"Shoot it," Harley answered.

Shiloh chuckled softly. "I think that might get me into some trouble."

"Slingshot?"

Shiloh laughed. "I couldn't hit the broad side of a barn with a basketball, let alone using a slingshot."

Harley opened one blue eye and looked at her girlfriend. "Well, you're no help at all."

Shiloh gasped, smiling as she did, and she pushed at Harley's shoulder. "How long has that tiny little feathered demon kept you awake?"

Harley sighed. "Two hours now."

"Well, that's not going to work." Shiloh glanced at the clock. It was four in the morning, and they needed to get up in two hours. "Let's try this." Reaching for her phone Shiloh pulled up an app she'd saved months before. She turned up the sound and hit play.

The sound of rain filled the room. "How's this?" she asked Harley, even though she could already see a blissful look cross her girlfriend's face.

"Oh, that's nice…" Harley murmured, reaching out her hand and gesturing to Shiloh's phone. "Gimme."

Shiloh chuckled, handing her the phone.

Harley touched the screen a few times, and suddenly the rain sound flowed through the speakers that were installed in the ceiling of every room in the house.

Harley sighed. "Oh, that's much nicer…"

"Show off," Shiloh muttered.

Harley chortled, knowing that Shiloh wasn't really annoyed.

They lay back down, and Harley was easily able to drift off to sleep.

"Well, who knew that would help?" Shiloh commented three hours later as they drove into work.

"What?" Harley asked, having been thinking about a program she was testing.

Shiloh smiled. "You not getting enough sleep."

"Help with what?" Harley was mystified.

Shiloh leaned over, looking at the speedometer on Harley's 370Z; it read sixty miles per hour. "Not getting enough sleep actually gets you to slow down." In response Harley pointedly sped up. "No one loves a smart ass, Harley Marie Davidson," Shiloh commented darkly.

Harley gave a bark of laughter. "Oh but babe, you do!"

Shiloh just shook her head. "Yes, yes I do."

***

"How cold do you think it is in Mexico in December?" Gray asked.

Rayden glanced up from the paper she was reading. "That was random."

Gray laughed. "I know, but I was just kind of mentally planning what I'd pack for the cruise."

"Honey, it's like ten months away," Rayden told her.

Gray made a sound in the back of her throat. "Yeah, and I may need to buy stuff that's winter like, and the best time to do that is in winter."

Rayden put down her paper, narrowing her eyes. "How is it that I can hear you rolling your eyes at me?"

Gray reached over to pat Rayden's hand. "'Cause you know me, sweetie pie!"

Licking her lips in mock incredulity, Rayden nodded her head. "Okay, I see how it is."

"Oh it's warm there!" Gray exclaimed, looking up from her phone. Obviously she hadn't even been paying attention to Rayden's show of false shock.

Rayden could only laugh and shake her head at her wife. "If you could look it up, why did you ask me?"

"Because you are wise, my darling." Gray smiled brightly.

Making a sucking sound through her teeth, Rayden narrowed her eyes at her wife. "You're lucky wolves mate for life."

Gray pressed her lips together, her eyes smiling at her wife. Getting up from her chair, Grayson walked over to where Rayden sat. She pulled the newspaper from her wife's hands, and straddled Ray's lap, putting her arms around Ray's neck. "But you love me."

Rayden gave her wife a considering look, pursing her lips. "Maybe…"

"Oh no, you love you, you know it," Gray assured her.

"Pretty sure of yourself, aren't you Mrs. Blackwolf?"

"Yes ma'am," Gray commented, her slate blue eyes staring down into her wife's dark eyes.

"You're kind of a brat," Rayden told her.

Grayson shrugged. "Mated for life, babe, you can't get rid of me."

Rayden laughed, moving to stand, holding her wife the entire time. Grayson wrapped her legs around Ray's waist as she was carried to the couch, her wife kissing her as she did. It was a lovely Saturday morning.

***

"I am not trying to get out of it," Memphis stated.

"Bollocks!" Kieran retorted.

"Kier," Memphis began, her tone reasoning, "I'm just saying they're asking me to do this, and it's probably going to happen in December."

"You don't even like Christmas movies!" Kieran complained.

"It's a revamp of Scrooge, it's a huge production, what am I supposed to say?"

"You're supposed to say, 'thanks, but not on your bloody life, I have plans with my wife!'"

Memphis had been asked to do sound for a live production of Scrooge for the Celebration Theater. It was a theater company that had been based in West Hollywood for twenty years, and was known for producing gay-themed plays. The theater was getting ready to move to a new venue in Hollywood, and wanted to kick of their season with a bang. They'd planned a gay/lesbian version of *A Christmas Carol*.

"But it's for the community!" Memphis called, as her wife strode away from her down the hall to their bedroom.

"Which would normally be wonderful, but you're going on this cruise, Memphis Lassiter!"

"Why?" Memphis asked plaintively as she walked into their bedroom and lay down on their bed. She looked up at Kieran who was hanging up her sweater, with jerking motions because of her annoyance. "Why do you want me to do this cruise so badly?" Her question was serious and sincere.

Kieran turned around, seeing the look on her wife's face and sighing immediately. She sat down on the bed. Placing her hand on Memphis's stomach, she felt the tension there. She knew what came next was Memphis throwing up due to that tension, and that would not do at all.

Kieran and Memphis had met through Memphis's friend and roommate Oliver, who had been trying to get Kieran's attention on a chat site. Memphis had stood in for him when he couldn't figure out how to get Kieran's attention. It had ended up being a longer-term task for Memphis, when Oliver couldn't seem to keep Kieran interested. Memphis had actually grown attached to the diminutive English woman over the course of their conversations. So when she'd come from London to visit and Oliver had been less than polite about Kieran not being the tiny skinny woman she'd looked like in her picture, Memphis had become enraged and had admitted to Kieran that she'd actually been chatting with

Memphis, not Oliver most of the time. The dye had been cast then, and Kieran and Memphis had become closer.

It had also been that time in Memphis's life when her past had come back to haunt her, and it had caused her so much stress, she'd been throwing up often. Fortunately, it didn't happen as much as it had previously, since their lives were very settled now, but it did still occur when Memphis got too upset about things. The last thing Kieran wanted to do was to be the cause of that tension. So she was very gentle with her next statement.

"Listen, love, I want you to do the cruise because I think it would be good for you to get back to doing what you love, while at the same time, getting back out into the world." As she spoke, Kieran slid her hand soothingly over Memphis's stomach, as if trying to physically quiet her concerns. "This cruise is a good opportunity for that. You'll be around people you are comfortable with, and our friends will be there too."

"People I'm comfortable with, meaning lesbians, right?" Memphis clarified.

Memphis had a lot of phobias about strange men due to her past.

Kieran smiled. "Yes love, lesbians."

Memphis chewed on her lip, her mind turning over and over what Kieran had said.

"And you think it will be good for me to get out? Have I been inside that much?"

Kieran pressed her lips together in consternation. "Yes, love, you have. It's beginning to worry me."

Memphis frowned. "I don't want to worry you."

"I know that, I know you're not doing it on purpose. I just think that your past, combined with your experience with getting COVID has just served to shroud you from the world."

Memphis's lips twitched and she thought about what her wife had just said.

"Kinda becoming a hermit, huh?" Memphis queried.

"Somewhat." Kieran nodded.

Memphis looked up at the ceiling for a long few moments, swallowing convulsively a few times, then finally nodded. "Okay, I'll do the cruise."

"Lovely!" Kieran clapped her hands. "And maybe tell the theater that you'd love to work with them on a different production."

Memphis nodded, smiling again. "You take good care of me, babe." She reached up, touching the curve of Kieran's cheek. "I love you."

"It's my job to take care of you, lovey." Kieran smiled, leaning down to kiss Memphis's lips. "And I love you as well."

Chapter 3

June 13, 2022

"No?" Cody sounding dejected already.

"Nope," McKenna said, her tone equally sad. "I was hoping, since my period hadn't started…" She did her best not to cry.

Cody stepped in to hug her wife. "It's okay, babe, it'll happen when it's meant to."

McKenna only nodded, not trusting her voice at that point. This was the third time they'd tried. Every time nothing happened. It was getting harder.

"Maybe we should look at invitro," Cody suggested.

"Doctor Hayes said we should try at least six cycles. Besides, invitro steps up the costs significantly." McKenna shook her head sadly. "I'm wondering if this is fate's way of telling me we shouldn't have a baby."

"No, bullshit." Cody made a cutting gesture with her hand. "If anyone deserves a baby it's you and me. We kill ourselves to make a difference in kids' lives every day."

McKenna took a deep breath through her nose, blowing it out slowly as she nodded. She felt like such a failure, why couldn't she do this? Why was she letting Cody down? In her head she knew that it wasn't her fault, she knew that the human body couldn't always be forced to do what was natural. She tried to block out all the rhetoric about it not being natural to do artificial insemination, that they were trying to do this the 'wrong way.' Unfortunately, her heart just couldn't accept what her head was saying at that moment.

"Maybe we should look into adoption," McKenna offered. Cody pressed her lips together, not wanting to say the first thing that came to mind at that idea. "What?" McKenna asked, recognizing Cody's gesture.

Cody scrunched up her face as she drew a breath in through her nose, blowing it out a moment later in a rush. "I would like the chance to have a baby that someone else hasn't already fucked up. You know?"

McKenna grimaced, knowing that Cody was referring to herself, since it was how she came to be part of a family. Cody had been a troubled kid, having been molested by her step-father. She had run away from home in the Midwest and come to Los Angeles. She'd met Dakota and they had formed a partnership on the streets, but when Cody had been arrested, she'd gotten lucky by being put in a children's home with Savanna. Her life had changed, but it didn't erase what she'd seen, done, or continued to see in her job; children messed up by their parents, or life in general.

Reaching over, McKenna put her hand on Cody's face. "I do know, babe."

"So we'll keep trying?" Cody asked.

McKenna nodded. "Yes, we'll keep trying."

Cody hugged her. "I gotta get to work." Leaning in, Cody kissed her wife. "You try to have a good day, okay?"

"I'll try."

"It takes time," Savanna said later that morning over coffee with McKenna.

"It didn't with you," McKenna pointed out.

"We were extremely lucky," Savanna admitted, "I know that. It will happen for you too, honey, you both deserve this."

McKenna smiled sadly. "That's what Cody said."

Savanna gave her daughter-in-law a sidelong look. "But you don't believe that, do you?"

McKenna shook her head.

"But why, honey?"

McKenna blinked a couple of times, looking like she was holding back tears. Savanna reached over and took McKenna's hand. "Tell me."

Holding her hands helplessly, McKenna sighed. "After all that stuff John did, I just wonder if this is Karma."

John had been McKenna's husband at the time she'd met Cody, who was undercover as a teenager in the home John ran. McKenna had been working on her internship for her degree in the home. Little had McKenna known that John had been trapping teenage girls in the home into a life of prostitution. It had been Cody who had gotten the evidence on John, all the while falling for McKenna. McKenna had been shocked when she'd found out that Cody wasn't a teenager, but an agent for the Department of Justice. While it was a surprise, it was also a relief since McKenna had found herself drawn to Cody.

Savanna squeezed McKenna's hand. "Baby girl, that's his Karma, not yours."

"I should have known," McKenna insisted.

"He was slick," Savanna told her. "He made sure you had no idea."

McKenna shook her head sadly. "Still, I should have seen it."

"You are going to make yourself crazy if you don't let this go, McKenna. You have to forgive yourself for believing that the man you'd fallen in love with was who he said he was."

Blowing her breath out slowly, McKenna did her best to take in what Savanna was saying. "It's amazing that we can help other people through this kind of stuff, but we can't help ourselves sometimes."

Savanna laughed. "That's why we have fellow psychiatrists, honey."

"I guess I got pretty lucky to have one that's my mother-in-law, huh?"

"Yes, you did." Savanna winked. "Just work on forgiving yourself, McKenna, I think you'll start to see things more clearly then."

"Thank you," McKenna reached over and hugged her mother-in-law. "I will definitely try."

***

Getting married in Mexico was more work than Raine and Natalia had thought. It had taken a serious effort to get Raine's birth certificate from New York, but then there were so many other hoops to jump through. It was daunting.

51

"Maybe we could just go to the courthouse here, and then do a ceremony there?" Raine offered after they'd run into another roadblock.

Natalia looked surprised by the idea, but after thinking about it for a few minutes, she finally nodded. "It might be the best idea."

There were too many things that had to be taken care of in Mexico, and they weren't sure how much time they'd have, since the cruise ship would only be docked there for one day. They didn't want everything rushed.

"Actually, come to think of it," Raine said, the idea settling over her more, "we could get married and stay around for a bit if you want. We could catch a flight back to LA from Puerto Vallarta."

"Stay around for a bit?" Natalia queried. "Cuanto tiempo es un poco?"

"A little bit, like maybe a few days, a week?" Raine suggested.

"That would be wonderful!" Natalia was overjoyed. She had been worried that she wouldn't have any real time with her family, so this was more than she could have hoped for.

Raine smiled, glad she'd made her fiancée so happy. Natalia all but danced over to her, hugging her tightly. "Gracias, mi amor. I love you."

"I love you," Raine replied.

It was amazing to think about how rocky the road for been for them at one point. After falling for each other fairly quickly, the two had moved in together. Things had been great, until the couple started drifting apart. When things had gotten bad, they'd split apart. Raine had been the one with the open and generous heart of forgiveness and it had brought them back together. It had been something that had made Natalia love Raine even more then and their bond was stronger than ever.

"Have you found the dress you want yet?" Raine asked a few minutes later. Natalia shrugged, looking away. Raine recognized the gesture. "Nat…tell me. What did you find?

"It's too expensive, I'm still looking," was the airy reply.

"How much is too expensive?"

Natalia pressed her lips together, looking away again.

"Come on carino, tell me," Raine urged gently.

"Too much," Natalia insisted. "I can find something else I like."

Raine considered for a moment, but finally dropped the subject.

***

"So what dress did Nat find?" Raine asked Jazmine the next day. She'd caught up to Jazmine at the studio after one of her classes was over.

Jazmine grinned. "She won't let you buy it, it's expensive."

"How expensive?"

Jazmine looked pensive, knowing Natalia would kill her if she told Raine about the dress. The dress had looked absolutely beautiful on Natalia and Jazmine had felt that it was a perfect mix of classic and modern for the tiny Latina dancer. Natalia had literally lit up with joy when she'd seen it, but tears had formed in her eyes when she'd found out how much it cost. It had broken Jazmine's heart to see her friend put the dress back.

"Raine…" Jazmine began, shaking her head.

"Just tell me, Jaz."

"Like thirty-seven hundred bucks."

Raine drew in a deep breath, somewhat surprised by the figure. But she felt that this was something that she needed to do for her fiancée. "She really liked it?"

"You should have seen her face, Raine, she was devastated at how much it cost."

"Okay, where did she find it?" Raine asked, all business.

"Love and Lace in Irvine. You're going to get it for her, aren't you?" Jazmine knew the answer already, but wanted confirmation.

"Duh," Raine replied simply.

Jazmine reached out and hugged the other woman. "I am so glad she has you."

Raine smiled. "We have each other."

"As it should be."

Two days later, Natalia arrived home from her night class at college; she was taking a couple of refresher classes to finally get her license to work with kids. Raine was in the kitchen cooking dinner, so she walked into the kitchen to kiss her.

"How was class?" Raine asked, as she chopped carrots for the soup she was making.

"Long!" Natalia exclaimed. "But I'm almost done, so it's okay."

"I understand that!"

"Do I have time to take a shower?" Natalia asked as she stole a carrot piece and popped it in her mouth.

"Plenty of time."

Natalia nodded, leaning in to kiss Raine again, then headed for the bedroom. As she walked in, she saw a large box with a bow on it laying on the bed.

"Raine! Que es esto?" she called as she stepped into the room, looking at the box.

"Open it." Raine said from the doorway to the room.

Natalia looked over at her fiancée, narrowing her eyes slightly. "What did you do?"

Raine shrugged, smiling smugly.

Natalia opened the box to find a card lying on top of the tissue paper. It read: "Para tu primera y unica boda" which translated to "For your first and only wedding." Opening the tissue paper, Natalia saw the bodice of the dress she'd found days before, but hadn't been able to buy.

"Oh Raine…" Natalia breathed, tears in her eyes instantly. "Que hiciste. ." repeating 'what did you do' in Spanish in her emotional state. Then she looked over at Raine. "Did you look at it?"

"Nope." Raine shook her head. "I told them what dress I wanted and your size and asked them to box it up. I didn't need that kind of bad luck." She winked on the last.

"Oh honey." Natalia's gaze fell on the dress nestled in the tissue again. "This is too much."

"No," Raine insisted, "this is our wedding, babe, and we're doing it right, the first and only time."

Natalia scrunched up her face, as tears started to fall in earnest. Raine walked over, taking Natalia in her arms, hugging her as she cried.

"You are so good to me," Natalia told her, her face against Raine's shirt. "No one has ever been so good to me."

"No one else has been me," Raine explained simply.

"That is the truth!" Natalia whispered vehemently.

"Maybe why you're marrying me?" Raine chuckled to lighten the mood.

"No, it's for your millions," Natalia quipped.

"I don't have millions."

"Uh oh," Natalia replied, wide eyed, then they both broke into laughter.

Natalia tucked the dress of her dreams away in the closet, hugging herself as she did, unable to believe she would get to wear such a beautiful garment on her wedding day.

It was a happy night.

***

"It's just a trip to the grocery store, why do I need to come?" Memphis complained.

"You said you wanted some things and I want you to pick them out," Kieran replied patiently.

"Like what?"

"Cereal."

"Anything will do."

"Really?" Kieran commented, narrowing her eyes. "Last time I bought you cereal you complained that it was too 'yucky adulty.'"

Memphis grinned unrepentantly. "Yeah, I did say that, huh?"

"Yes, you also complained that the fruit I picked out wasn't sweet enough."

"Oranges have to be smooth, babe."

Kieran tilted her head slightly. "And this would be what I mean."

Memphis slumped her shoulders. "But it's so peoplely out there!"

"Yes, love, but it's early at the moment, so if you'd stop giving me a rough time, we could go before all the people come out."

"Fine," Memphis practically moaned.

At the store, Memphis put one headphone in her ear, leaving one headphone dangling down and turned on her music. It was a coping mechanism; Kieran was used to it.

As they shopped, Memphis's head would bob to a song, or she'd sing a lyric she particularly liked. All the while Kieran continued shopping. Kieran did notice that people looked at them oddly; Memphis was dressed in tattered jeans, black and white Converse, and a black hoodie with the hood up, with white-blonde spikey hair sticking out. Conversely, Kieran was dressed in a pink and white tracksuit and white tennis shoes. They were polar opposites.

At one point, someone stopped them, having recognized Memphis. Kieran noticed the two steps back Memphis took. Fortunately, the fan also noted Memphis's discomfit and toned down their approach.

"I just wanted to tell you that I thought your album was amazing," the fan said, smiling at Memphis.

Memphis nodded, licking her lips in tension. "Thank you."

"I'm sorry to bother you, I just couldn't pass up meeting you," the fan said, biting her lip, her eyes glassy from unshed tears.

Something clicked in Memphis then she realized she'd made the girl feel uncomfortable, and she didn't like that she'd done that. Smiling, Memphis nodded her head.

"It's okay, I just got COVID a couple years ago from a fan who grabbed at me," Memphis explained.

"Oh, I'd never presume to touch someone I didn't know," the young woman said, sounding appalled.

"Well, that's good." Memphis smiled again, her look much warmer now. "This is my wife, Kieran."

"It's nice to meet you," the woman said with a friendly smile.

"Lovely to meet you as well," Kieran told her.

"So, could I bug you for an autograph?" the young woman asked, holding up her grocery list and a pen to Memphis with a soft laugh.

Memphis outright laughed. "Sure, what's your name?"

"Laura."

Memphis signed the grocery list with "Great to meet you, Laura!" and signed her name with a comical flourish.

Laura canted her head. "Is that Linkin Park you're listening to?"

"Yep." Memphis nodded. "Actually, it's Mike Shinoda with Fort Minor right now, but essentially Linkin Park."

"I started listening to them after I heard that song you did for Remington LaRoché."

"Well, have you heard of Fort Minor?" Memphis asked, warming to her favorite topic.

Kieran leaned in. "I'm going to keep on, you two have a nice chat." She kissed her on the cheek. She was inordinately pleased that Memphis was actually chatting with a stranger, and she wanted to give her a chance to do that without feeling like she was holding up the shopping.

Memphis grinned. "I'll catch up."

"Yes, you will." Kieran winked. "Good to have met you," she told Laura and walked on down the aisle.

Twenty minutes later, Memphis caught up to her wife in the cereal aisle. She looked very happy.

"So how many bands do you have her turned onto now?" Kieran asked.

Memphis laughed. "Just a few."

Kieran noticed that Memphis's hood was down, a sure sign that she was much more comfortable now. "The bands should be paying you royalties for all the fans you send their way."

"Nah, the joy of music is to share it," Memphis told her.

It was a good day.

***

"What did you do?" Dakota asked her girlfriend as she noted the ice pack on Jazmine's knee when she came in the door that night.

59

"Oh, I really pissed it off today with a jump," Jazmine told her as she leaned up to kiss Dakota hello. "How was work?"

"Same shit, different day." Dakota smiled. "What's for dinner, is it something I can help with?" she said, gesturing to the ice pack.

Jazmine sighed. "I just need twenty minutes with this, and I can handle it."

Dakota looked considering for a minute. "Let's just Door Dash it, babe, that way you can rest."

"Are you sure?"

"Yes, babe, I'm sure," Dakota assured her, picking up Jazmine's laptop from the nearby table and handing it to her. "Order whatever you want, you know what I like. I'm gonna jump in the shower."

"Okay, thank you." Jazmine nodded gratefully. She'd been dreading having to get up to make dinner. Standing didn't sound like a great idea yet.

An hour later the food arrived and they sat eating with the TV on. Dakota was looking through emails on her computer, and Jazmine had switched to heat for her knee.

"Should we have that checked out?" Dakota asked, reaching out to touch Jazmine's knee gently.

Jazmine shook her head. "No, I think it's okay. I just tweaked it a bit."

"Okay, but if it hurts too long..." Dakota's voice trailed off as she read an email. "Well, holy shit."

"What?" Jazmine queried.

"Cassandra is getting married."

Cassandra was a woman that Dakota had dated, who'd been rather controlling, and who'd seriously injured Dakota at one point. Later she'd done her best to make it up to both Dakota and Jazmine by buying a Craftsman house, and selecting Dakota to restore it and paying handsomely for the job. She'd then turned around and given it to the couple as an apology for her previous behavior.

"Really? Is it Salina, that artist she was dating?"

"Yep, looks like it, and we're invited to the wedding."

Jazmine canted her head. "Is that a little weird though?"

"In the lesbian world?" Dakota shot back.

"True!" Jazmine laughed. "Where is the wedding?"

"Dunno yet, this is just the 'Save the Date' announcement thing."

"When is it?"

"Frigging Christmas Day." Dakota shook her head.

Jazmine chuckled. "Well, I guess we'll just see."

"I guess so. We don't have to go, you know."

"I know, but it could be interesting." Jazmine lifting her eyebrows a couple of times.

Dakota laughed. "Oh shit!"

***

"Nope, we're going to have to reshoot that." Legend shook her head, looking disappointed. She'd been reviewing the dailies from the movie she was currently shooting.

Sandy grimaced. "I'm not sure we can get the location again this soon."

"Make it happen," Legend told her, undaunted.

"BLM isn't always that fast."

"The Bureau of Land Management needs a kick in the butt then." Legend smiled.

"It's going to be getting hot now, not cold as fuck like it was out there before," Sandy reminded her.

"That's why they're actors," Legend shot back.

The movie was being filmed in Monument Valley, Arizona and getting the permit to film on Navajo land wasn't a quick process. Regardless, Sandy got to work on doing the request.

"Aren't you being just a little bit picky?" Riley asked later that evening after reviewing the footage Legend wanted to reshoot.

"The lighting is wrong," Legend commented.

"The lighting is fine."

Legend narrowed her eyes at her wife. "Are you a director?"

Riley narrowed her eyes right back. "No, I'm an actress, which means I'm the victim of an overly difficult director."

"Meaning?"

"Meaning, some damned director doesn't like one tiny nuance, and I'm having to haul my cookies all the way back from whatever location I'm currently filming on. Then I'm having to get back into whatever character I was in at the time of that movie. I have to put myself back into that mindset, taking away from the mindset I was building for the current film I'm working on. It's a pain in the ass, and it's damned disrespectful to not only me as the actress, but also to all the people I'm working on my new film, including the new director."

Legend's mouth dropped open in shock at the diatribe, then she closed her mouth, her lips curling in self-depreciation. "Let me look at it again."

Riley sat back, pushing the screen back to Legend. The director watched the clip three more times. Finally sighing.

"Okay, you're right, I just needed to watch it again."

"And again, and again," Riley added, smiling to take the bite out of her words.

Legend leaned in kissing her wife, pulling back to look her in the eyes. "Thank you for giving me perspective."

"Thank you for listening." Riley sighed.

Legend had always been a perfectionist on her films. On the one hand it was an admirable quality, but on the other it could really hinder an actor or actress. There were a lot of type A personalities in the film industry, but it took someone with a certain amount of humility to be able to listen when they were told about what their foibles caused others. Riley was proud to be married to someone who could be reasoned with. She knew it wasn't always the case. It did make her feel special that Legend would hear her when she needed to.

***

"How many bikinis are you going to buy?" Rayden asked patiently as she watched her wife picking up various suits.

"Probably one for every day of the cruise," Gray told her with a sly smile.

"Great…" Rayden murmured.

Gray walked over to her wife, putting her arms up around her neck, smiling up at her. "You don't like seeing me in bikinis?"

"Sure, if I'm not having to beat off every other lesbian on a damned cruise ship." Rayden smiled beatifically as she said it.

"Oh honey, you'll be sitting there with a lovely scowl on your face, no one is going to be brave enough to come near me. They'll be too afraid of my Cherokee warrior."

Rayden pursed her lips, giving her wife a scowl. "You're just evil."

Grayson nodded. "Sometimes, yes, yes I am."

"I hate to mention it, but we do need to pick up something for Nat and Raine's wedding too."

Raine and Natalia had recently announced that they were planning to get married in her hometown when the ship stopped in Puerto Vallarta. They were stunned when all of their friends said they would be showing up for the wedding. McKenna and Jazmine offered to help get things together for the wedding, and help out the day of.

"Aw damn! And a gift!" Gray added.

"We're giving them money for a gift."

Gray shook her head. "That's terrible."

"But it's what they need and want," Rayden told her.

Gray sighed. "Could we at least put the cash in something pretty?"

"Like what?" Rayden asked suspiciously.

"Let's go look!"

They were at Bloomingdale's in the Beverly Center Mall. Gray took Rayden upstairs, and they perused the glassware.

"This! This is it!" Grayson said, picking up a vase. It was decorated with vivid colors of orange and purple on it.

"Gray, that damned thing is nine hundred bucks!" Rayden exclaimed loudly.

"Shh!" Gray told her wife, even as people around them glanced over.

"I think that's a little much," Rayden added, her voice lower this time.

"But it's so pretty…" Gray sighed. "It looks just like Natalia to me."

Rayden pressed her lips together. "Cash won't fit in it."

Gray smiled brightly. "A check will."

Rayden shook her head. "You're killin' me honey."

"I know, but you love me, and you love Raine and Nat too."

"Not nine hundred bucks worth," Ray muttered under her breath as Gray motioned to the salesperson. She picked up the pretty vase; it had a graceful curve to it, like a dancer. "Damned thing weighs a ton," Rayden said. "Raine better not piss Nat off."

"Ray!" Grayson cried, even as she laughed.

The salesperson approached the women, her eyes taking in the height of the dark-haired Rayden. She was indeed a formidable looking woman, with her strong Cherokee features. Grayson noticed the saleswoman looked a tad intimidated.

"She's harmless," Grayson joked, gesturing to her wife behind her.

The saleswoman, whose name tag read Jan, gave a wan smile. Then her eyes turned to the vase Rayden was handling. She reached forward to take it out of Ray's hands, clearly afraid Rayden would damage the item just by touching it.

"This is a Kosta Boda vase from the Orchid Collection," the woman said, her voice a bit haughty. "It's nine hundred dollars," she informed them, as if saying it was millions.

Gray and Rayden exchanged a look, it was obvious the saleswoman didn't think they could afford something so expensive. Rayden's visage darkened significantly.

"I see," Gray said with a bright smile, "what would you suggest?"

Jan gave them a wintery smile. "We have some lovely Rosenthal vases over here," she told them, walking toward a much cheaper section of the house goods. The vases she pointed out to them were significantly cheaper at forty-five dollars. It was obvious from her sneer that she thought it was all they could afford. The vases looked like something that had been previously shattered and glued back together haphazardly.

Gray looked up at Rayden with a curl to her lips. Rayden raised one dark eyebrow, looking at Jan. "Those look like someone had a rough time with glue."

"I assure you they're very fashionable," Jan went on undaunted.

"Let me rephrase," Ray said, her dark eyes sparkling with malice, "they look like shit."

Jan gasped at the use of profanity. "I beg your pardon."

"Don't beg," Grayson said, leaning back against Rayden, her arms crossed in front of her chest. "Just go get us another salesperson please."

Jan looked completely affronted, but scampered off.

"The nerve!" Grayson raged when she'd gone.

"Some people just never get past the exterior, babe," Rayden commented.

"Hi! Can I help you?" asked the saleswoman that Jan had sent over.

Rayden gave a slight smile. "Hopefully."

"Your co-worker seemed to think this would be our best place to find a vase for our friends who are getting married," Grayson told the younger woman. "What do you think?"

Marla looked surprised, then she shrugged. "I'm sure anything you like would be perfect." Then she leaned in conspiratorially. "Jan's kind of a stick in the mud, you know?"

Rayden chuckled, even as Grayson put her arm through Marla's. "I think we're about to make your day." She led Marla back over to the Kosta Boda vase. "This is what we want to buy."

Marla smiled and nodded. "Absolutely, I'll get you one from the back that's in the box. Would there be anything else?"

"Just that I sincerely hope you work on commission here." Grayson smiled.

"We don't, but our sales numbers are how we get raises." Marla winked at the couple.

"Fabulous!" Grayson enthused as she and Rayden followed Marla to the cash register.

Jan all but swallowed her tongue when she saw Marla ringing up the Kosta Boda vase. It was definitely worth the view for Rayden and Gray.

***

"We need to get something to wear to Natalia and Raine's wedding," Shiloh reminded Harley.

Harley glanced over her shoulder at Shiloh and sighed. "Do we have to do that today?"

"We have to do that before we forget," was the answer.

Harley nodded, finishing up the line of code she was writing. Shiloh walked over to where Harley sat at her home computer.

"You know, you are supposed to do this stuff at work," Shiloh told her. "Not on Saturday."

"I know, I know, I just need to get this piece done. I want to present it to Gage on Monday."

Shiloh leaned down, kissing Harley on the neck. "I'm making coffee, it's obvious you've been up for a while." Harley gave her a guilty look. "I don't even want to know! But you will be in the kitchen for coffee within the next hour."

"Yes ma'am." Harley smiled.

An hour later, Harley joined Shiloh in their backyard with her coffee in hand. Shiloh looked down at her watch, a beautiful silver Movado with a rainbow crystal bezel on the face, a gift from Harley. "Right on time."

"I know when not to be late." Harley laughed. "So where do you want to go to buy something for the wedding? And what are we getting them for a gift?"

"Clothes wise, probably Beverly Center. Gift is money."

"Isn't that tacky?" Harley asked as she took a bite of the toast Shiloh was eating.

"That's what they're asking for, so that's what we're getting them."

Harley curled up her lip. "Can we do both?"

Shiloh smiled brightly; Harley had the most generous soul. "Of course we can do both."

"Okay." Harley nodded. "But you pick, because you know me, I'd just give them a laptop or something computer related."

Shiloh rolled her eyes and laughed. "Yes, I know. I'll see what everyone else is doing. I seriously doubt any of our friends will stick by the 'just money' rule."

"Probably not," Harley agreed. "So what time to you want to go?"

"After I fix you a proper breakfast," Shiloh said, smacking Harley's hand as she reached for her toast again. "And then we can shower."

"Yes dear," Harley murmured.

Later at the Beverly Center, the couple planned to separate to go looking for their clothes.

"You sure you don't want to check out Dolce and Gabbana?" Harley prompted as they looked at the directory.

"I am not paying that kind of money for a dress!" Shiloh insisted.

"Okay, okay." Harley laughed. "I'm headed to Banana Republic up on seven."

"I think I'll go to Bloomingdale's, looks like I'm on six. Text me if you change stores, I don't want to wander all over the mall looking for you."

"Yes ma'am." Harley grinned.

Harley had been known to wander away from where she'd originally been headed. Shiloh would spend awhile trying to find her.

At Bloomingdale's Shiloh zeroed in on a dress fairly quickly, it just took a while to get a fitting room to try it on. In the end, she selected a navy blue cocktail-style dress from BCBGMAXAZRIA, with a beautiful corseted bodice, an asymmetrical tiered skirt and spaghetti straps. She texted Harley to let her know her dress was navy blue, so Harley could hopefully coordinate. When she didn't hear back from Harley, she immediately worried that she had meandered away yet again. Life with a woman with ADHD was always an adventure!

Fortunately, the first thing Shiloh did was check the store Harley was supposed to be in: Banana Republic. She walked around the women's section, not seeing her girlfriend. Passing by the dressing rooms, however, she heard some girl laughing loudly. That immediately made her curious, so she headed toward the dressing rooms. There stood Harley, holding clothes on her arm, and standing in front of her was a sales girl. Shiloh could tell by the way the girl kept reaching out to touch Harley on the arm, and the way Harley looked like she was trapped, that girl was doing her best to flirt with the blonde programmer.

70

"There you are!" Shiloh exclaimed, walking over to Harley, reaching up to kiss her lips soundly. "Thanks for helping her," she said to the girl, looking at the name tag, "Marie, but I have it now."

It was obvious from the girl's face that she was surprised, but apparently she wasn't ready to give up either. Marie looked past Shiloh to smile at Harley. "You just let me know what other things you want to try on and I'll help you."

Harley looked alarmed at the possible battle brewing, and Shiloh made a point of walking Harley over to the largest dressing room. "We need this one please."

The salesgirl was smart enough to walk over and unlock the dressing room, but when Shiloh stepped inside with Harley, she insisted, "I'm sorry, you can't go in with her. It's store policy."

"Yeah," Shiloh said, "I don't care." With that she shut the door in the girl's face.

When Shiloh turned around, Harley was grinning at her.

"What?" Shiloh asked. "She was being a snot."

Harley licked her lips nodding, her look gleeful.

"Shut up," Shiloh grinned, "just try on the suits."

Ten minutes later, Shiloh was admiring her girlfriend; they'd walked out to the main mirrors s they could see the suit from all angles. It was a nicely cut, and fit Harley perfectly. It had a single button blazer, with pants that were boot cut, which were great, since Harley always wore dress boots. They suit was a heather grey, which went perfectly with Shiloh's dress.

"This is the one, babe," Shiloh told Harley.

"That looks fantastic on you!" Marie said from the doorway to the dressing rooms.

Shiloh, who was still facing Harley with her back to Marie, rolled her eyes. "What do you think, babe?"

Harley looked in the mirror, turning her head this way and that. "Yep, I like this one."

"Great! Go ahead and change, and I'll deal with getting it rung up," Shiloh told her.

Harley hesitated, worried about what could happen if she left Shiloh alone with Marie, but she knew she had no choice, so she went to change. Once out of the suit, she handed it to Shiloh over the dressing-room door, and Shiloh made her way to the cash register. At the register, Marie walked up, standing by as Shiloh paid. Shiloh was sure she was trying to make sure that her name was mentioned as the person that helped them.

Once the transaction was finished, Shiloh added the bagged suit to the dress over her arm. Marie moved in as she turned to go back to Harley.

"I hope you don't think I was flirting with her," Marie said.

Shiloh shrugged. "Wouldn't matter if you were, Harley doesn't cheat."

Marie canted her head. "You sure about that?"

"Yes, she is," Harley put in, standing behind them.

Marie's eyes widened. "I...I'm..."

"You're done," Shiloh said, taking Harley's hand and walking out of the store. "I swear," she said, looking up at Harley, "I can't leave you alone for even a minute!"

Harley chuckled. "And apparently I need to keep an eye on you before you become a brawler."

***

"What's with your boots?" Lyric asked Dakota.

Dakota glanced down at her work boots with Pleasing Peach still lingering on them, then sighed heavily. "A kid at the job site…it's a long story."

"How's it going now?" Cody asked.

"With Ski? She's been working with the drywall guys, fetching mud and tape and stuff. Not too many calamities to be had there."

"So who is this?" Savanna asked, as she set mashed potatoes on the table.

"She's a young woman that was hanging out panhandling in front of the studio," Jazmine told them. "Dakota told her she'd be better off getting a job."

"Dakota!" Savanna exclaimed. "That wasn't nice."

"I gave her a damned job, didn't I?" Dakota shot back.

"Easy…" Lyric put in, not liking Dakota cussing at her wife.

"I'm sorry, Mom," Dakota said immediately, reaching over to kiss Savanna on the cheek.

Savanna and Dakota had developed a bond early on. Dakota had been very different then; she'd been very rough emotionally. It had taken Savanna's gentle way to soothe Dakota's turbulent soul. They'd been very close since then.

"It's okay." Savanna smiled. "So this girl had a mishap?"

"She's had almost nothing but mishaps," Dakota clarified.

"Not the least of which was getting paint dumped on Dak," Cody commented, her grin barely hidden.

"Ya know…" Dakota began, walking toward Cody.

Cody laughed, holding up her hands. "Okay, okay!"

"Don't make us separate you two," Lyric said, something she found herself saying often when her two daughters were in a room together. Luckily, Anastasia, the youngest, always seemed to bring out the best in her sister.

"No fighting!" Ana told the two women, standing between them imperiously.

"Yes, ma'am." Dakota smiled.

"I wasn't fighting." Cody grinned. "Sister was, I was just defending myself."

"Sister!" Ana exclaimed, her hands on her little hips, staring up at Dakota.

"Well, give me something else to do!" Dakota laughed, picking up her little sister.

"It's time to eat, ladies," Savanna put in.

"Well, that solves that," McKenna added.

"For now," Lyric told her daughter-in-law.

***

"Children should be allowed to express themselves freely," Wynter stated.

"As long as they're respectful about it," Remington added.

74

The two had been discussing their parenting philosophies, wanting to make sure they were on the same page on how children should be raised.

"Define respectful," Wynter replied.

Remi looked back at Wynter for a long moment, trying to decide how to define something that was so ingrained in her. "There's a difference between expression and outright defiance, cheri."

"True," Wynter said. "How would you feel if our child turned out to be gay?"

"I would be sad for them."

"Sad?"

"Look at the world as it is." Remi gestured to the news showing on the TV. "It is not a good time to be different."

Wynter drew in a deep breath, blowing it out as she nodded. "Maybe we'd be able to shield them from that."

"There is no way to shield a child from everything."

"I know," Wynter commented sadly. "Doesn't mean I wouldn't try."

Remington smiled. "And that is what I love about you."

"Any ideas when you want to start trying on this?" Wynter twisted her wedding ring unconsciously.

Remington noticed Wynter's gesture, and reached out to take Wynter's hands in hers. "When would you want to begin?"

Wynter pressed her lips together. "Would the beginning of year be crazy?"

Remi smiled indulgently. "Not at all."

Wynter leaned over to hug her wife, excited by the prospect.

Chapter 4

Cruise Day

"Holy Hell…" Dakota exclaimed as she and Jazmine boarded the ship.

"You are not kidding," Jazmine whispered.

The Zaandam was a beautifully appointed ship. With an incredible lobby featuring a three-story high ornate pipe organ right in the center, and an equally impressive twenty-foot Christmas tree standing right next to it, decorated in a beautiful nautical theme. Ornaments of turquoise and white varied from starfish to crabs to seahorses. It was festive and very impressive with twinkling lights and iridescent icicles.

Cody nodded toward the organ. "Get a load of that."

"That's wild!" McKenna gasped in astonishment.

"You're holding up the works there, Falcos!" Rayden called from behind them. "Move it along."

"Blah, blah, blah…" Dakota called back to Ray, laughing all the while.

"Don't make me come up there, Dakota," was Ray's response.

Dakota moved along, quickly.

The group quickly discovered the turquoise and white Christmas theme was carried throughout the ship. Trees of various sizes, ornaments, garlands, and wreaths adorned doors, walls, and railings everywhere. It was magical.

"Here are your staterooms," the hostess, who had introduced herself as Gianna, gestured toward the door. "We reserved the Pinnacle Suite staterooms for you, as they are a best and biggest." She opened the door to the first suite. "Ms. Kincade, we have you and your wife in here…"

"Oh mwen…" Remington breathed as she gazed at the enormous room, decorated in golds, browns, and shades of red. "Sa a bel."

"She says this is beautiful," Wynter translated helpfully, "and she's right, this is fantastic. Thank you so much."

Gianna smiled, surprised at how humble and down to earth the two major celebrities seemed to be. She'd expected attitude and rudeness, as she'd experienced with other stars on other cruises.

"I'll let you get settled." Gianna nodded. "The company left you this, to thank you for sailing with us." She gestured to the huge gift basket and champagne on ice.

Wynter's eyes widened at the basket that stood a good two and a half feet tall. "Wow, that's amazing too. Thank you."

"Our pleasure," Gianna said sincerely.

She showed Legend and Riley to their suite across the hall.

Gianna smiled. "Our other Pinnacle Suite."

Legend beamed. "Now this is what I call some serious digs."

"It is definitely sailing in style," Riley agreed. "I've been on multimillion dollar yachts that weren't this well appointed."

Their suite was also decorated in golds and browns, with blue as the accent color.

"I think ours is cooler." Legend grinned mischievously.

"Yeah!" Riley chimed in, laughing.

Gianna laughed too, definitely liking these stars this trip.

"If you'll come this way, we've reserved a Neptune Suite for you." The girl whose name was Cindy led them down the hallway. "I'm sorry, we ran out of the Pinnacle Suites; my co-worker beat me to them." This was said with a bright smile.

"It's okay," Memphis said, rubbing her nose with her index finger. "They're real stars, they should be in the best rooms."

Cindy stopped walking. "Now, hold on here," she said, putting her hand out in halting motion. "I think you're a pretty big deal." When Memphis looked skeptical, she went on, "Oh, no, no, no, you're amazing! I've seen you spin! Oh my God, it was so awesome! And that album you did, was so good. I absolutely love it! As far as I'm concerned, you're a musical god."

Memphis's eyes grew wider and wider as Cindy spoke. A grin tugged at her lips when the girl made the comment about being a musical god.

"Tell us how you really feel, love," Kieran added into the silence that ensued, her eyes sparkling with joy that this girl was praising Memphis so much.

"Yeah, stop that hemming and hawing." Memphis winked.

Cindy laughed nervously. "I'm really not supposed to say all that, but I was just so jazzed when I heard I was getting to escort you to your room." She began to walk again, stopping at their stateroom and opening the door.

"This is great!" Memphis nodded, looking around the room.

The room had a king-sized bed, and nice sitting area with a fridge.

"The best part is here," Cindy said, walking over to the window and opening the curtains, exposing floor-to-ceiling windows and a small private veranda.

"Boy howdy," Memphis murmured.

"Oh!" Kieran enthused. "It's lovely! Much bigger than I'd have expected on a ship."

Cindy smiled. "I'm glad you like it. The company also left this for you." She gestured to a gift basket and champagne, much like Wynter and Legend had received in their rooms.

"Wow…" Memphis breathed.

"Ace!" Kieran added.

Later, the group got together in the Ocean Bar for a nightcap. It was already eight p.m. They'd had an early dinner in San Diego, where they'd met the ship.

"How's everyone's room?" Rayden asked, lifting a beer to her lips.

"Ours is amazing!" Wynter enthused.

"Yeah, you got one of the super cabins," Dakota told her. "Big star and all."

"Hey, we took the cabin they gave us," Wynter said.

"They are super nice though," Riley put in. "How is everyone else's?"

"I'm completely happy with ours," Raine said. "It's not huge, but we have a partial view of the ocean."

"Shi scored us one with a full view of the ocean and, amazingly, the Wi-Fi does not suck here." Harley grinned.

"We got a pretty cool room," Memphis said.

"I'm good with ours," Dakota said, glancing at Jazmine who nodded in agreement. "We even got one right next to Cody and McKenna."

"What about yours, Ray?" Legend asked.

"It's great...the bed is a little short." Rayden laughed.

"Anything but a king sized is too short for you, babe," Gray told her.

"True." Ray nodded.

"Guess you'll just have to spoon." Dakota winked.

"Watch it, Falco," Rayden commented. Dakota only laughed.

"Everyone up for meeting for breakfast, around eight?" Legend asked the group.

The group agreed, and shortly after everyone retired for the night.

Breakfast the following morning was buffet style in the main dining room. The room itself was two stories and beautiful. The food was abundant and everything one could possibly want to eat.

As a group of sixteen, the girls took up some space, but they'd been put in a reserved area so they could eat in peace. There had already been a few fans of Wynter, Legend, and Riley asking for autographs. Some of the braver butch women had even asked Remi for an autograph.

"This food is amazing!" McKenna exclaimed as she dug into her pancakes with fresh fruit.

"Right?" Jazmine agreed. "There's so much fresh fruit!"

"So good!" Natalia chimed in.

"What's on the agenda for today?" Shiloh asked.

"I'm spinning at Club Hal and Oasis at noon," Memphis said.

"Well, then the pool it is." Gray smiled.

Later at the pool, there was a major stir among the lesbians on board when Wynter and Riley walked out. They shook a lot of hands, and signed more than a few hats and even a few boobs. One of the deck hands showed the ladies to the area that had been reserved for them, to keep them from being mobbed. Legend and Remi also caused a stir, but they had drinks in both hands, theirs and the ladies, so they weren't pestered for autographs.

When Memphis appeared above the pool at her DJ stand, the crowd went wild. She smiled and waved as she donned her headphones, leaving one off her ear.

"Good afternoon, ladies!" Memphis called. "Let's jump right in here!" She immediately cut in a dance beat that had the crowd dancing and pumping their fists.

The rest of the group had joined Wynter, Remi, Legend, and Riley in their area, each with their own drinks.

Wynter canted her head at McKenna. "You don't look so good. Are you seasick?"

McKenna grimaced, nodding. "I didn't really think I would be, on a boat as big as this, but I used to get seasick on my parents' boat. I brought Dramamine, so hopefully it'll kick in soon."

Wynter gave her friend a sympathetic look. "I'm sorry."

"Here babe," Cody said, handing McKenna a cup. "I finally found some Ginger Ale."

"Thanks." McKenna took it gratefully.

"This one is for my friends," Memphis announced from her spot. "A little Clean Bandit featuring Zara Larsson."

The song began, and the words really sounded right for all of them. The lyrics talked about hearing symphonies instead of silence and how this person was the one that had set them free with their love. The chorus requested that she hold her tight and not let go.

The crowd cheered as Legend leaned in to kiss Riley, feeling the music.

After the song ended, Memphis started out with "I Kissed a Girl" by Katie Perry, which had everyone cheering. Then she mixed in "Born This Way" by Lady Gaga. The crowd went absolutely wild when she mixed in "Petrified (Los Angeles Remix)" by Fort Minor. It was a harder core rap song, mixed with rock that talked about everyone being so "petrified" by them, and that they should just step aside. The entire time the song pumped through the speakers Memphis pointed down at her friends.

As the song ended, Memphis was back on the mic again. "I don't know if all of you know, but we've got some serious OGs on this boat! We've got Rock 'n' Roll Goddess Wynter Kincade, movie star icon Riley Taylor-Azaria, and her awesome director wife, the movie god, Legend Azaria, and last but never least we've got all-time MMA champion, Remington LaRoché!" The crowd screamed, whistled and cheered. "I'm lucky enough to call all of these amazing women my friends! Now, I know you're dying to see all these heavy hitters up close and personal, but please remember they're human beings too, and need their space."

"We love you Memphis!" one woman screamed out. That was followed by all kinds of screams and cat calls.

"I love all of you too," Memphis said, holding her hand to her heart humbly. "But my heart belongs to my lovely wife, Kieran! Give them a wave, babe!"

Kieran shook her head in embarrassment, but waved to the crowd.

Someone yelled out, "We love you too, Kieran!" which made everyone burst into laughter.

"Now let's get back to it!" Memphis yelled. It was indeed a fun afternoon.

Before Memphis's set ended, however, the head purser for the boat announced a 'lottery' of sorts to win the chance to have breakfast with Memphis. This completely shocked the DJ, who looked alarmed at Kieran. She held up her hands in futility, she hadn't known anything about it.

"Now, it's only for ten of you, so everyone put your entries in this afternoon, and we'll draw tonight at dinner."

The crowd went wild. Memphis breathed a huge sigh, but nodded to Kieran, indicating she'd be okay.

"Don't forget," the purser went on, "tomorrow night we've got Wynter Kincade performing on the mainstage, you don't want to miss that! And the next morning we have the panel of all of our awesome stars for a question and answer session!"

That night at dinner, Wynter, Remi, Legend, Riley, Memphis, and Kieran were asked to join the captain's table. The captain, a woman named Larissa, was very charismatic and chatted happily with the six ladies.

"I'm so looking forward to your show, Ms. Kincade," Larissa enthused.

"Please call me Wynter, I'm looking forward to the show too. It'll be great to play such a cozy venue for a change."

"The panel should be interesting too, with the five of you. So many interesting women and stories from what I've heard!" She looked over at Memphis. "And I understand there was a breakdown in communication with you, Miss Lassiter."

"Memphis, please," Memphis indicated, taking a deep breath and blowing it out she nodded. "Yes, there was a little problem, but I think it's going to be okay."

The captain smiled, her bright eyes lowered for a moment. "I appreciate your indulgence, I believe my purser just got a little ahead of herself. It was an idea, only, from me, and she just ran with it, thinking it was a request. I'm sorry she didn't check with you both first."

"It's alright," Kieran told her.

She and Memphis had talked about it, and Memphis felt sure she would be okay, since it was only ten women. It had definitely been a shock to her system, but she'd recovered quickly. Kieran imagined it was because she was still on her high from DJ'ing for the first time in a long time.

That night the ten winners were picked, and breakfast was set for nine the following morning.

***

Memphis was up before dawn the next morning. She kissed Kieran and told her she was going down to the fitness center. Predictably, Remi was already there working out.

"Good morning." Memphis murmured as she stepped onto the treadmill next to the one Remington was on, putting her headphones in.

"Bonjou, piti." Remi smiled, calling Memphis little one.

Remington had formed a bond with the slightly built DJ during a concert tour with Wynter. Remi had become one of Memphis's protectors when she was having issues with the cult she'd escaped from during her childhood.

The two worked out together in relative silence, although Remi could hear the music pumping through Memphis's headphones, and knew she was stressed.

After a shower and some coffee, Memphis was getting ready for the breakfast she was dreading. Kieran noticed her wife's discomfort and knew she needed to be alone for a little bit.

"I'm going to head down to the venue to check things out," Kieran told Memphis, kissing her on the lips. "Come down when you're ready."

"Got it," Memphis said. She was standing in the bathroom doing her hair.

Kieran didn't comment on the fact that Memphis's hands were shaking.

At the Explorations Café where the breakfast was being held, Kieran noted that four fans were already waiting outside, even though there was still a half an hour before the event was to begin. Kieran saw a perfect opportunity.

"Good morning, ladies." Kieran smiled at the women.

"You're Memphis's wife, right?" a dark-haired woman asked.

"Yes, I'm Kieran."

"I'm Rebecca, it's great to meet you." The woman smiled warmly.

Kieran nodded. "Ladies, can I ask you a favor?" She leaned in conspiratorially.

"Of course!" A woman with blonde hair exclaimed.

"Well, you see, my wife has been through a lot in the last few years, not the least of which was getting COVID from a fan that got too excited and grabbed at her while sick with the virus."

"Seriously?" another woman commented.

"Right?" the fourth woman in the group said. "What do you need from us?"

"Can you please spread through the group this morning to just be a bit reserved until Memphis warms up to this event? She's used to being separate from the crowd, and she's not big on being in public these days."

Kieran's request was met with comments like, "Of course!" "Totally get it!" "For sure!" She went into the venue, feeling much better about the situation.

As Memphis emerged from her cabin she noted that Remington and Rayden stood outside waiting for her.

"I, uh, wow." Memphis grinned. "Are you two acting as my bodyguards this morning?"

"Indeed," Rayden said.

"Wi madam," Remington added.

Memphis felt a lump rise in her throat; her friends always protected her. It was a good feeling, but also emotionally overwhelming at that moment, so she nodded her head, smiling in thanks. As she walked down the hallway, Remi and Rayden fell in behind her.

When they reached the doors to the Café everyone was seated inside. She was met by the head purser.

"Ms. Lassiter, I'm so sorry that we didn't check with you on this, that was my fault. I really appreciate you doing this." The woman looked so overwhelming grateful that Memphis didn't have the heart to say anything about the lack of notice.

"It's okay. Let's do this," Memphis said, nodding.

The doors were opened and Memphis was hailed with a small standing ovation. The room was arranged so that there were two larger round tables of five women each, and a smaller round table where Memphis and Kieran sat in front of the two tables. It was cozy, but not too close. Memphis noted other round tables that had been pushed off to the side, and suspected her wife had something to do with the rearrangement.

With Remi and Rayden behind her, Memphis walked through, shaking hands with the women, thanking them for coming. All the while her two dark angels kept watch over the crowd to make sure no one made Memphis nervous. Kieran quickly arranged for a bigger table that could also include Remi and Rayden.

During breakfast, women started asking Memphis questions.

"What got you into DJing?"

Memphis took a sip of her coffee. "I love music, I discovered that early on, and DJing was a way to be around music all of the time."

"Don't you have a degree in music?"

Memphis grinned, it was weird that people knew this much about her. She never did interviews, so anything that was released was either speculation or came from BJ Sparks himself.

"I do, it's actually in Audio Production, but yeah, it's all about music."

"How did you and Kieran meet?"

Memphis laughed at that question. "I'm going to let her answer that one."

Kieran looked very serious for a moment. "She catfished me." This caused a shocked gasp, but then laughter as Kieran started to smile. "Honestly, I thought I was talking to a man her friend Oliver but since he wasn't able to keep my attention on his own, Memphis sat in for him a few times."

"Then it became a lot of times, when I was on tour with Wynter and Xandy Blue," Memphis added.

"And before I knew it, I was in love." Kieran smiled wistfully.

The group collectively said, "Aww."

"You're Remington La Roché, aren't you?"

Remi inclined her head.

"Are you Memphis's bodyguard?"

"Memphis is a friend, I love her dearly, and will protect her against anyone," Remi said simply.

"Who is your other bodyguard, Memphis?"

"That's Rayden." Memphis smiled. "She's a badass too."

Rayden laughed at the description. "I'm a friend of hers too."

In the end, the breakfast was a rousing success. Memphis signed lots of autographs, and was pleasantly surprised at how respectful people were of her space. She suspected that somehow her wife had everything to do with that.

***

"This is the life." Raine sighed, her face turned up to the sun.

"Si lo es," Natalia commented with a sigh of her own.

Raine smiled. "This is like a pre-honeymoon."

"Carino, this is the honeymoon."

Raine didn't say anything, only smiling up at the sun.

***

That night at dinner, the group all got to sit together.

"So, who's up for ziplining at our first stop?" Cody asked.

"I'm in!" Dakota held up a finger.

"Me too!" Harley nodded.

"I think I'll try it," Gray put in.

Rayden smiled. "That means I'm going too."

"I'm going Christmas shopping," Riley said.

"I'm with Riley!" Wynter chimed in.

"Me too!" Shiloh crowed.

"If Ri is going, so am I." Legend sighed.

"I'm in as well." Remi nodded.

"You bois don't have to…" Riley said, feeling bad that Remi and Legend now had to go with them.

"You aren't going anywhere without protection, babe," Legend told her.

"Agreed," Remi said, giving Wynter a meaningful look.

"Yeah, but…" Wynter started to vacillate.

"It is fine, mon amour," Remi soothed. "If I am with you, I am happy."

Wynter pressed her lips together. "Okay, thank you. But the next stop we do what you want to do."

Remi inclined her head. "Absoliman."

"I like that…" Legend said, her voice trailing off ominously as she looked at her wife.

"Oh shit," Riley muttered, causing everyone to laugh.

In the end, Cody, Dakota, Harley, Ray, Gray, and Raine went ziplining, the rest, except for Memphis and Kieran went shopping. Memphis and Kieran stayed on board and enjoyed a quiet afternoon by the pool.

"I'm not sure this is a good idea…" Cody commented, as they put on her harness.

"If I'm doing it, you're doing it," Dakota said as she stood on the next platform over, having her harness hooked up.

"Okay, but if we die, the moms are going to be really mad." Cody chuckled.

As they got ready, the women helping them communicated with the other side of the zip line.

"Two coming over, they're sisters, don't let them die," said the girl working with Cody with a wink.

"Their moms will be mad," said the girl working with Dakota, grinning all the while.

"Okay," Cody's guide said, "get ready, hold on up here." She showed Cody the handles above her head. "When you're ready, just move into a sitting position and go."

Cody heard Dakota's guide tell her the same thing. "Ready sis?"

"Yep!" Dakota called back.

"One!" Cody yelled.

"Two!" Dakota yelled back.

"Three!" they said together and both went to the cheers of the rest of the group.

The air was cool on Cody's face, and she looked around the sea of green leaves below and around her.

"This is awesome!" she heard Dakota yell.

"Woohoo!" Cody answered.

They were caught on the other side by two more women, and Cody wondered mildly if Olivia Cruises insisted that only women be on their excursions too.

Next up were Raine and Harley.

"You jump, I jump!" Harley called to Raine.

"Then let's go!" Raine yelled, moving to the sitting position and pushing off. "Holy shit!" she yelled as she flew past trees.

"I love it!" Harley exclaimed.

Last up were Rayden and Gray.

"You're not going to chicken out on me, are you?" Ray asked her wife.

"I'll beat your ass there," Gray countered.

And so she did! It was a great experience for all of them. They arrived back at the ship, having done the zip line three times each, happy and famished. They immediately hit the bar for drinks and snacks.

***

Shopping went off, for the most part, without a hitch. There were a few times when someone recognized either Riley or Wynter or both. Fortunately, Remi and Legend were there to keep people from mobbing their wives. Regardless, many presents were bought and tucked away.

They all arrived back at the boat a couple hours after the others, with a few hours to spare for Wynter to get ready for her show.

***

That evening, after a quick dinner, Wynter went on stage, but with a much simpler version of her concert shows. She played a number of the crowd favorites, and one that she always played, a cover of Queensrÿche's "Hand on Heart" for Remi. It was a song she'd started performing after Remi had saved her life on stage. As always, it drove the crowd wild, especially when Remi walked on stage to meet her wife with a dozen red roses.

The show was, as always, a hit! Afterwards, Wynter was gracious enough to sign multiple autographs. By the time she had showered and crawled into bed beside Remi that night, she was happy it was her only show. Other than the panel the next evening, she got to relax the rest of the cruise.

The next day, the ship docked in Puerto Vallarta, Mexico. The group sat at breakfast making their plan for the day.

"Fishing trip!" Dakota announced.

"Same!" Rayden chimed in.

Wynter looked over at Remi. "You're gonna make me go fishing, aren't you?" Remi pressed her lips together, raising her eyebrows a couple of times to indicate that yes she was. "So, yay, fishing," Wynter said unenthusiastically, even as she grinned at her wife.

Legend tilted her head and Riley in question.

"As long as there's wine, and I can bring a book, I'm in," Riley pronounced.

"Then we're in," Legend chuckled.

"I'm not going near a smaller boat at this point," McKenna said.

"Still having seasickness?" Wynter asked.

"The Dramamine helps, but sometimes it gets ahead of it in the mornings." McKenna shrugged.

"There's a swim with seals and dolphins excursion that I want to do," Natalia said.

"Oh, I'm so in on that," Jazmine agreed.

"Me too," Raine added.

"Dolphins!" McKenna called. "I can definitely handle dolphins."

"Seals!" Kieran said.

"I'll go fishing," Cody said.

Gray looked conflicted, but put a conciliatory hand on her wife's arm. "I'm sorry, babe, but I'm swimming with mammals."

Rayden chuckled. "I knew you'd stay away from yucky fish."

"And worms!" Gray made a barfing gesture, sticking out her tongue.

"I think I'll go fishing," Memphis said, surprising everyone. "What? A chance to hang out with the bois!" She laughed at the astonished looks on her friend's faces.

"Harley? Bros or hoes?" Dakota asked.

"Hey!" Shiloh smacked Dakota's arm.

Dakota just laughed unrepentantly. "I'm sorry, ladies."

Harley looked Shiloh. "What do you want to do, babe?"

"Swimming with dolphins sounds fun," Shiloh responded.

Harley nodded. "Then that's what we'll be doing."

With that decided, everyone finished breakfast and went back to their cabins to get ready for their activities.

***

The bois ended up on a smaller boat with three other women. Riley and Wynter got comfortable on the bow with books and wine. They were joined by one of the three women whose friends were on the boat as well.

"Thank god you ladies are here!" the woman, who'd introduced herself as Jan, said. "I was not going to be putting anything on a hook!"

"We're with you," Wynter agreed.

"Oh, my god you're Wynter Kincade...and you're Riley Taylor. Well, this is just a treat!" Jan said, smiling from ear to ear. "I promise I'm not a rabid fan or anything. I just think you're both so fabulous!"

Riley and Wynter smiled, appreciating Jan's friendliness.

At the stern of the boat, the shit talking was already starting. One woman, Jess, was a good old-fashioned butch from the good old days. She shook hands with the other seven. "Good to meet ya," she said with a wide smile.

"Hey, I'm Del," the other woman said, inclining her head to everyone.

The bois introduced themselves.

Both women recognized Remi with nods and comments about her being a great fighter. They also recognized Legend and Memphis. There were comments all around.

"Okay, so now that we're all introduced, let's get going," Jackie, the boat captain said, steering the boat out of the marina. As she drove the boat she talked, "So the fishing here is commonly for Sailfish, Dorado also known as Mahi, Mahi. We have Yellowfin Tuna, big fuckers those, Wahoo and Mako sharks. Since it's December, you might even have a shot at a Striped Marlin. Who here are experienced fishers?"

The two women not with the group raised their hands.

"I've fished in rivers back home," Rayden said. "Never done ocean fishing though."

"Where's home?" Jackie asked.

"North Carolina," Rayden answered.

Jackie nodded. "But you're used to baiting hooks and all."

"Yes, ma'am."

"Anyone else?"

The rest shook their heads.

When they reached their fishing site, Jackie went about showing the newbies how to bait their hooks and how to work the rod and reel. She also showed them how to cast out their lines. Once the lesson was done, everyone got their line out of their area of the boat.

There were some chuckles when Memphis had made a series of faces as she tried to put a bait fish on her line. Remi had stepped in to help her, having been a quick study.

There was excitement when Cody managed to hook a Wahoo, also known as a Pacific Kingfish or ono. It took her a few minutes to reel it in, but once she did, Jackie commended Cody, "That's a good sized one! 'Bout a twenty pounder! Do you want to keep it? We can have it cleaned and packaged for you?"

"Sure!" Cody said, smiling excitedly.

Others caught fish as well, but the most excitement was when Rayden actually hooked a Striped Marlin. It became a battle of wills to reel the huge fish in. At one point the marlin jumped out of the water on the line.

"Holy shit that's a monster!" Dakota yelled.

"You got this, Ray," Remi encouraged.

By this time, Rayden was seated on the "fighting chair" with her feet braced on the step designed for the purpose. Remi stood behind her, at the ready to help if needed. The fight was definitely on! It took Rayden twenty-five minutes to reel in the fish, but it was a beautiful moment when she eventually got it on board.

"You're getting this guy stuffed and mounted, right?" Jackie enthused.

Rayden gave the large fish, who was fighting for breath, a knowing look and shook her head. "Can he still live if we release him?"

Jackie looked stunned, but nodded her head all the same. "Because you got him in fast, yes."

"Then it will be," Rayden said.

"Let's at least snap a picture, huh?" Jackie encouraged.

"Quickly," Rayden agreed.

"Good call, my friend," Remi told Rayden, understanding that Rayden didn't like to kill any living being she didn't need to; it was part of her heritage.

The rest of the trip was fun with the others catching smaller fish.

***

"This is so cool!" Jazmine crowed, as she was able to pet a seal that swam up close to her.

It had been a process to get into the water with the mammals they'd all had to shower and don life vests. They'd been instructed what to do and not do around the seals and dolphins, but now they were in the water and loving every moment.

Natalia smiled softly as she pet a dolphin, and it just felt very intimate, like she was connecting with the animal. Raine watched her, and snapped a few pictures with the waterproof camera she'd bought. She was so happy they'd been able to make this trip. It had been a wonderful time for them.

Harley and Shiloh were petting a dolphin that had swum over to them as well and were loving it.

"They're just so sweet," Shiloh said She was almost in tears because she was so happy.

Harley was thrilled to see Shiloh so happy.

"He won't bite me, yeah?" Kieran asked the woman who was working with her and one of the seals at the encounter.

"No, just move slowly," the woman encouraged with a smile.

"You got this, Kieran," McKenna encouraged.

"Oh my god, they are fantastic!" Gray whispered excitedly.

The girls had a great time, feeding and petting all of the dolphins and seals. Afterwards they had a few drinks at the bar while they waited for the boat to take them back to the ship.

"I've never been so close to a wild animal before!" Kieran exclaimed.

"Me either," Jazmine said, grinning lopsidedly. "Unless you count some of the men I dated before."

Everyone laughed at her comment.

"How do you think the bois are doing?" Shiloh asked.

"Memphis texted me this picture," Kieran said, showing the picture of Memphis with her fish.

"Dang!" McKenna cried. "That's pretty cool, but icky fish."

"Well, my woman got the king here," Gray said, showing the picture Rayden had sent of her with the Marlin.

"Whoa!" Raine yelled. "That's some fish!"

"Damn girl! You got a provider there," Jazmine told Gray.

"She released it." Gray smiled.

"Seriously?" Natalia asked.

Gray had a soft look on her face when she said. "It's her way." The other women shook their heads. Gray shrugged. "She's Cherokee, her people don't take a life that they don't need, for food, for their family, or tribe."

"That's beautiful," Natalia sighed.

"Yeah, it really is," McKenna agreed.

Harley nodded. "Very cool."

"Definitely cool," Shiloh seconded.

Dinner that night was a cacophony of discussions about fish, dolphins, and seals. After dinner they went to the dance club, where Memphis was eventually coaxed into doing some DJing. After a while, some of the group made their way to the Zaandam Casino to enjoy some slots and poker. It was a lovely night on the ship.

The day of the panel arrived; Legend, Riley, Wynter, Memphis, and even Remington were all taking part. The discussion was held in the mainstage room, since so many women on the ship wanted to be there. The MC of the panel walked out onto stage, bowing to the women sitting at a table on the stage.

"Thank you, ladies, for being here, I'm Janice and I'm going to be your host tonight." The MC smiled at the panel, then turned to the crowd. "Do these women rock our world or what?" The crowd cheered and stomped their feet. "Now I'm going to jump right in, and because I'm MC I get to ask the first question!" Turning to the panel, the woman smiled again. "I understand that you're all friends in this big world we live in today, how does that happen?"

The group chuckled amongst themselves.

"Well," Legend began, looking at the group for their agreement that she start them off, "I got to meet these ladies when I made a movie with Riley. They were friends long before I got there. I have to say it's probably the second-best thing I've done in my life in recent years, next to meeting Riley."

"I met the ladies of our group when a friend, who isn't here on this cruise, introduced me to her friends. I had come to California when I retired from fighting. That's when I met Wynter," Remi said.

"And I met Wynter and Remi when I did my first concert tour for Badlands Records," Memphis added.

"But there's a larger group of you, right?" Janice asked.

"Yes," Wynter said, pointing out the rest of their group sitting off to one side, "but there's more at home, we just didn't want to take up every room on the boat." She winked at that last part.

"And you all hang out together?" Janice clarified.

"A lot, yes," Wynter confirmed.

"Are there any other famous people in your group?" Janice queried.

"Some of you might have heard of Xandy Blue," Legend said. "And her wife, Quinn Kavanaugh."

"Aw, the white knight." Janice nodded. The crowd went wild again.

"Our other famous friend is Sable Sands, although we don't see her as often, because she and her wife live in San Francisco now," Riley said. "Most of the rest of them are heroes in their own way, though, either as first responders, or ex-military."

"I've done movies of a few of their lives," Legend added in.

Janice looked appropriately impressed. "You women really do rock the world, don't you?"

The group laughed.

"Okay, who else has a question?"

One woman raised her hand and was given a microphone. "Yeah, I just want to know where the hell I need to move to, to hang out with y'all!"

The crowd burst into laughter and clapping ensued.

"We're mostly in West Hollywood."

"Aw, WeHo girls, huh?" Janice commented. "Who's next?"

"This question is for Legend," the next woman said. "What you said about Georgette at the end of your movie *For the Telling*, was that really true?"

Legend nodded. "Yes, ma'am, it was absolutely true."

"I so loved that movie!" the woman called.

Legend inclined her head. "Thank you."

"This question is for Remington," the next person said. "What got you into MMA fighting?"

Remi looked thoughtful for a moment. "Well, while I was in the Marines"—a cheer went up from the crowd—"I realized I was fairly good at hand-to-hand combat. So once I was discharged, I decided to give boxing a shot. It wasn't the same, but a promoter saw me, and told me I should get into MMA. That is what I did."

"And you're damned good at it!" the woman responded.

Remi pressed her lips together and inclined her head graciously.

"My question is for Wynter. Were you two dating before Remi saved your life?"

Wynter chuckled. "No, I was still with my ex-girlfriend then. But it definitely showed me what I was missing."

Remington had been filmed as she'd talked to Wynter, trying to keep her awake. It was something Wynter hadn't remembered until it was played over and over again in the media.

"I fell in love with her gentle ways and protective streak," Wynter continued, winking at Remi, who only smiled softly.

"My question is for Riley," an older woman said. "You always dated men before, did you ever suspect that you were gay?"

Riley shook her head. "No, ma'am." Her eyes fell on Legend. "It was as if playing Georgette, and her falling in love with Legend made me do the same."

"There was a lot going on behind the scenes that people didn't really know about too," Legend added.

"Like what?" the woman asked.

"Like drug use and a suicide attempt on my part," Legend commented. A gasp rippled through the crowd. It was something

102

that hadn't ever been released before. Legend's admission had Riley reaching out for Legend's hand, squeezing it gently. "Riley was there for me every step of the way." It was obvious from the look Legend gave her wife that it was the reason she'd fallen in love with the actress. "Her deciding to be gay, was just a bonus," she added with a crooked grin.

There were many more questions, and before long the two hours they had set aside for the event passed. Even as the MC tried to wrap it up, people kept raising their hands. The panel agreed to continue for another half hour, showing the crowd at the event what true stars looked like. It was a great evening for everyone involved.

***

The ship was still abuzz the next morning about the panel the night before. Many people stopped by the group to thank Wynter, Remi, Legend, Riley, and Memphis for their candid answers. Many commented that they were even bigger fans now.

The ship was going to be pulling into Mazatlán later that day, and the group would be going ashore to make the forty-five-minute drive to El Quelite, Natalia's hometown. Raine and Natalia had been surprised that the rest of the group had insisted on accompanying them to Natalia's hometown. Not only that, but they were staying for the wedding as well.

"Before we get off this ship, I am getting a massage!" Gray stated emphatically.

"Oh, a massage sounds good," Natalia commented.

"Yes please," Shiloh said.

"Same, same," came McKenna's reply.

"Over here." Jazmine held up her hand.

"I'm hearing a trend…" Legend said, as she saw Riley nod. "Okay, all the girls want to go get pampered, so we bois can go do some water sport games before we dock. Who's with me?"

And so was spent the last part of their cruise.

Chapter 5

Arriving in Mazatlán, the group got organized and off the ship with the help of the ship staff, who had come to really like the ladies; they tipped well, and were exceedingly kind and appreciative of everything that they had done.

At the dock, Wynter had arranged for a Hummer Limo to meet them to drive them to El Quelite. Natalia and Raine were completely shocked.

"Wynter, thank you so much…" Natalia, who was near tears at the generosity, said, hugging the superstar.

Raine extended her hand to Remi, and then to Wynter, thanking them.

"Everybody pile in!" Wynter encouraged.

The drive was fairly short, giving the girls time to chat, and relax. As they pulled into town, everyone oo'ed and aa'd over how beautiful it was. The main street's buildings were painted in bright yellows with beautiful magenta bougainvillea growing against them.

"I'm hungry," Dakota said, having seen a couple of restaurants.

"Me too," Cody said.

They hadn't eaten lunch on the ship, because they'd been too busy getting their items together to take with them.

"We should stop for lunch," Legend said, looking over at Natalia. "Are you okay with that?"

Natalia smiled, nodding. "I don't want to overwhelm my parents with this many hungry people."

"What about that place?" Gray asked, pointing out a restaurant with a grand-looking entrance.

Natalia shook her head. "Too flashy, their food isn't as good as their décor. I know a place." She gave the driver directions.

A few minutes later they drove up to an unassuming-looking beige brick building. The name on the sign read Los Arrieos. The group piled out of the limo, and walked into the restaurant, causing a bit of a flurry.

"This is beautiful," Kieran whispered, looking around.

"So pretty!" Jazmine agreed.

The interior of the restaurant was painted a bright shade of yellow, much like the buildings lining the streets. It had exposed wood-beamed ceilings and old pictures and various paintings on the walls, and color tablecloths on wood tables. It was rustic and gorgeous.

Once they were seated, everyone looked to Natalia to help them order. She obliged by ordering plates of various foods, so that everyone could share. The wait staff kept bringing food for what seemed like forever, but the group enjoyed every dish. Legend picked up the tab for lunch, and tipped handsomely.

"I don't think I can eat again for a week," Wynter commented. "That was so good, Nat, thank you so much!"

"My pleasure." Natalia smiled. "Thank you, Legend, for lunch."

There was a round of thank yous as they climbed back into the limo.

They continued on to outside the main part of town, stopping in a rural area. Natalia was practically vibrating with excitement to see her family. She was the first out of the vehicle when it came to a stop. She had called her parents from the restaurant telling them that they would be there within twenty minutes, so her parents were waiting for her.

The group watched as Natalia ran straight into her father's arms. Miguel Marquez was a big man, even at fifty-four he easily picked up his daughter, holding her in obvious jubilance as her mother, older sister, and brother jumped up and down in celebration. It brought tears to more than a couple of eyes. It was obvious Natalia's family had missed her.

When Miguel put Natalia down, she turned, extending her hand to Raine, motioning excitedly for her to come to her. The rest of the group stayed back, allowing the major introductions to happen without interruption.

"Mama, Papa, esto es Raine," Natalia told them, her eyes shining with tears of joy.

Raine stepped forward, extending her hand to Miguel. "Es un placer concerte." Her accent was perfect, so was her Spanish, and she could tell immediately that she'd shocked Natalia's family. Miguel's face lit up at hearing this red-headed white woman speaking his language so well.

"Es excelente concerte, Raine." Miguel shook Raine's hand emphatically.

Natalia's mother stepped forward. She was an older, heavier version of Natalia. "Soy Maria." She introduced herself, taking Raine in her arms and hugging her tightly. "Estoy tan feliz de concerte." She told Raine she was so happy to meet her.

"Raine, this is my sister Emilia and my brother Miguel Jr."

Raine smiled, nodding at both, but they both stepped forward to hug her at the same time, causing laughter all around.

The rest of group walked up then, and Natalia told her parents, "Estos san nuestros amigas," saying that they were their friends. Introductions were made all the way around.

"Come inside," Maria told them in heavily accented English, gesturing toward the house.

The home was a modest one story, with a small courtyard in front, stone floors, with colorful rugs all over them. The living room was arranged in two sitting areas with wood furniture covered in intricate carvings. Legend immediately began examining the detail as the others looked at pictures on the wall, and spoke with Natalia's family.

Miguel walked over to where Legend stood checking out a high sofa table. "You like?"

Legend nodded. "It's beautiful."

"I make this," Miguel proudly stated, then gestured all around the living room.

"All of this?" Legend clarified.

"Si, all."

Natalia walked over to her father, hugging his side. "My father is a carpenter. He makes furniture, shelves, he also does cabinets, and the occasional wooden toy." She winked up at her father.

"Ah, si, si." Her father nodded smiling.

"Your work is amazing, sir." Legend smiled.

Natalia translated when her father canted his head. He inclined his head to Legend in response.

"He sells furniture in town," Natalia told Legend. "My mother does pottery that she sells in town too."

"Very artistic family," Riley, who'd come up while they were talking, said. "No wonder you're such an artist."

Natalia smiled proudly. "I come from great artists."

They all sat out in the backyard later that day. It was a small oasis with a bougainvillea-covered pergola, and two beautiful mosaic tile fountains bubbling near the double French doors. There were wooden benches and chairs covered with red-and-yellow cushions all around the back patio. Even so, Miguel and his son had brought out dining room chairs to make enough seating for the group. It still wasn't enough so, Dakota, Cody, and Memphis all sat on the floor as they talked. Legend had said that they were young enough to be able to get back up off the floor without putting their backs out, which had caused a good laugh.

"Dondé esta la abuela?" Natalia asked her parents.

"Ella esta en la ciudad en el hospital para in el chequeo," her mother told her.

Natalia nodded, looking relieved. "My grandmother is actually in the city today getting a check-up. She got very sick during the pandemic."

"Memphis y Remington tambien se enfermaron mucho de COVID," she told her parents, telling them that Memphis and Remi had also gotten really sick during the pandemic.

"Pero ellas estan bien ahora? You are better, si?" Maria asked, looking at the two women.

"Yes, gracias." Memphis nodded.

"Yes," Remington said.

Miguel nodded, telling them through Natalia that the pandemic had hit the Sinaloa area hard, and that many people had been sick. There were over ten thousand deaths, and their small town was hit really hard due to the lack of tourists coming through.

Maria added that children had been left without parents, parents had lost children, whole families had died. "Fue devastador."

"It was devastating," Natalia translated.

The group was quiet for a bit, contemplating all that had happened in the last two years. While America had been hit hard, they still had a good infrastructure with which to treat people. It was hard to fathom how hard areas as rural as this had been hit.

"It really makes you think," McKenna commented, "how lucky we got."

Wynter glanced up at Remi, squeezing her hand that was clasp in her wife's. "We really did."

"Yep." Legend nodded, hugging Riley closer to her.

"Let's talk about happier things," Kieran suggested. "The wedding!"

"Absolutely!" Gray agreed, sensing the mood was going downhill quickly.

Talk turned to the wedding which was scheduled for the next day at the church in town.

Maria told Natalia that the priest who'd baptized her as a little girl was willing to perform the ceremony even though Raine wasn't technically Catholic. There was a lot of excitement and, when Miguel broke out the tequila, much toasting and drinking.

Fortunately, Wynter had booked them into the local hotel, the Hotel Villas Quelite, and the limo was waiting to take them there. They stopped on the way through town to grab Quelite's version of fast food and took it to the hotel.

In their room later that evening, Natalia lay in Raine's arms in their bed.

"Are you excited for tomorrow?" Raine asked.

"Yes!" Natalia laughed. "Are you nervous?"

"Nope." Raine shook her head. "I'm much more nervous about meeting your abuela."

Natalia smiled brightly. "She will love you."

"I hope so."

Natalia hugged Raine, snuggling her head onto Raine's shoulder. "How could she not?"

***

The morning of the wedding, a very nervous Raine was introduced Rosa, Natalia's grandmother, who didn't speak of word of English. The three met at a café for breakfast.

"Estoy tan feliz de concerte, querida," Rosa said to Raine, calling her dear, her dark eyes shining brightly. At seventy-seven she was still quite spry and spirited. "Creo que cuidaras bien de mi nieta." She told Raine that she thought Raine would take good care of her granddaughter.

Natalia's eyes sparkled with unshed tears. "She knows about Julie and how bad she was to me," she explained to Raine.

"Prometo cuidar bien su corazon," Raine told Rosa, promising to take good care of Natalia's heart.

Rosa patted Raine's hand smiling and nodding happily. "Ella esta en buenas manos."

Natalia put her head on Raine's shoulder. "I know I'm in good hands too."

That afternoon Natalia stood in the dressing room waiting for her father to come get her to walk her down the aisle. She reflected on the fact that Raine had been so thoughtful, wanting to get married in Natalia's home town. Since Raine was an orphan, she had no family, other than their friends, to be at the wedding, but for Natalia having her family there meant so very much to her, and Raine knew that.

The church was already decorated for Christmas; a large Christmas tree stood in the foyer, decorated in the traditional red and green colors. Hand-carved ornaments adorned the tree, and colorful, lit poinsettia stars hung across the foyer. Natalia enjoyed seeing the church she grew up in decorated as it always was. It reminded her of how happy she'd been there. Now she was marrying the love of her life there. It seemed so perfect.

With her arm in her father's, Natalia walked down the aisle toward Raine in the beautiful gown Raine had bought her. It was a Rish dress, a style called Yara. It was a vision of cream with a semi-sheer corset bodice made of floral lace. It had straps that were off the shoulder, almost like a tiny shawl, and gave her a romantic, dreamy look. Her long dark hair was swept back into a high elegant loose bun with flowers like those on the dress pinned in it. She carried red roses in a bouquet.

"Wow…" Raine breathed, standing next to Dakota who was standing in as a witness.

Dakota chuckled quietly, nodding her head in agreement.

Raine wore a grey suite with a bright white shirt and a slim charcoal grey tie; her long red curly hair was pulled into a long braid down her back.

"You look so handsome," Natalia whispered when she reached Raine.

"You are a goddess," Raine replied with a smile.

The ceremony was short and sweet, concluding with their vows.

"Since the day we met, I've known you were the one I wanted to be with," Natalia told Raine. "No one has ever been as kind and gentle with me as you have. I will spend the rest of my days just trying to show you how much you mean to me."

"Mi querida," Raine began, calling Natalia her darling. "You have shown me what love is, and what it means to share my life with someone else. You take care of me and give me everything I need, every day. Thank you for being the home I never had."

There wasn't a dry eye in the church that afternoon.

The reception was held on the outdoor patio of a restaurant called El Meson De Los Laureanos that was down the street from the church.

"Well, this was fun," Memphis commented. The party was winding down and the group were taking some time to relax and reflect on their exciting week.

"Even though you didn't want to come on the cruise?" Kieran raised an eyebrow at her wife.

"Yes." Memphis rolled her eyes. "I was wrong, you were right." The group laughed.

"This was a fun holiday," Riley said.

"Christmas is just two weeks away," Legend reminded her.

"Ugh," Riley groaned, "don't remind me, I still have shopping to do!"

"Does everybody have plans?" Cody asked.

"I have some thoughts," Remi said, grinning mysteriously at Wynter.

"What?" Wynter asked, looking suspicious.

"We'll talk," Remi said.

"Sounds ominous," Dakota commented.

"Trankil ou," Remi said.

When Dakota looked lost, Wynter said, "She told you to be quiet."

Cody laughed. "Good luck with that."

"Shut up," Dakota replied.

"Make me," Cody retorted.

"Alright you two," Rayden said, narrowing her eyes at the sisters. "Don't make me conk your heads together."

Cody and Dakota subsided quickly.

Raine and Natalia made their way over to the tables everyone was sitting at. Raine sat down in an open chair, and pulled Natalia down on her lap.

"There's the happy couple," Rayden said, smiling.

"Congratulations you two," Gray said holding up her glass of champagne.

"Congratulations!" everyone chimed in, holding up their glasses.

***

After leaving Raine and Natalia to visit with Natalia's family the next day, the group decided to check out some things along the route back to Mazatlán. They checked out historic sights, and McKenna even dragged the group to check out a children's home in town. It was a sobering sight, seeing so many children in need. Before they left, Legend and Riley, and Remi and Wynter both made large monetary donations to help the home care for the children better.

After a day of shopping and lunch in Mazatlán, they all headed to the hotel they had planned to stay in before heading home the next day. They met at the hotel restaurant for dinner. As dinner was winding down, Cody stood up suddenly. Everyone stopped talking and looked at her.

"So, here's the thing," Cody said, with an odd grin. "Apparently McKenna wasn't seasick on the cruise…"

"I'm pregnant," McKenna announced.

The table burst into a cheer, with everyone laughing and congratulating the couple.

"Merry Christmas to us," Cody told McKenna, hugging her close, her eyes shining with unshed tears.

"And then some," McKenna added, smiling brightly. They were happy to have finally managed to get pregnant, but it had also been a surprise for them. They'd done another round of insemination three weeks before the cruise, but when McKenna had started spotting just before the holiday, they'd assumed it was another failure, so hadn't bothered with a test. McKenna had started to suspect that she might be pregnant when her "seasickness" hadn't gone away the last couple of days. They were beyond thrilled and couldn't wait to get home to tell Lyric and Savanna.

The next day, the group flew back to San Diego, only to find that their Los Angeles flight had been canceled when they arrived.

"Well, son of a..." Dakota muttered.

"This sucks," Cody said, looking up the next available flights.

"Looks like midnight," Harley commented, having been searching for flights too.

"I see one at eleven, but it's only got three seats left," Rayden said.

"This totally sucks," Memphis grouched.

"I have an idea..." Legend said, working on her phone as a grin spread across her face.

Half an hour later, a shuttle bus dropped them off at Enterprise Rental Car.

"Bleh, rental cars?" Dakota said. Cody shrugged her shoulders. "I guess it's probably faster than waiting for flights." It was only two hours to Los Angeles from San Diego.

A woman walked over to Legend with a clipboard in hand.

"Right this way, Ms. Azaria."

The woman led them out a side door and into a parking lot where a series of sports cars were parked.

"Oh…" Dakota practically sighed. "They're so pretty!"

Legend gestured to the cars. "The Maserati Granturismo is mine, but the rest of you get to pick."

"So cool!" Cody yelled, as she ran straight toward one of the two Audi R8s.

"I'm getting the other one!" Dakota yelled, running for the other Audi.

Remi strolled casually to the Aston Martin Vantage.

Rayden picked a Mustang GT. "Had one when I was younger." She winked at her wife.

Memphis went for a Dodge Challenger RT with a Scat Pack.

Harley picked a Corvette, used to low-slung cars.

Legend signed for the cars, thanking the woman as she led Riley over to the Maserati.

Inside the cars, the group discovered radios tuned to the same station.

"Last one home is a rotten egg," Legend called over the radio.

And the race was on!

Epilogue

That year, instead of celebrating Christmas in the traditional way, Remington had asked Wynter if she'd be willing to accompany her to Haiti, where Remi's family was from. In August of 2021 on top of the COVID pandemic, Haiti experienced a 7.2 magnitude earthquake that damaged or destroyed over 130,000 buildings and left hundreds of thousands homeless. Over 2200 people had been killed.

After hearing about what had happened in a small town in Mexico, Remi had begun to worry about her own home country. For that reason she wanted to visit and see what, if anything, she could help with.

They arrived in Haiti two days before Christmas. They toured various reconstruction projects, and it was easy to see how much more was still needed to be done. It didn't take long before the press heard about their visit, and before long, cameras were following them everywhere they went.

At one point, they visited an orphanage, where children who had lost their parents were being cared for. The children were excited to meet celebrities like Wynter and Remington.

"Bonjou!" Remington called to the group of children gathered in one of the playrooms.

Many of the children called back, "Bonjou!" Remington walked around the room, talking to the children, as Wynter talked to the woman who ran the center, Marie.

"This is wonderful what you are doing," Marie said to Wynter.

"We just wanted to see what was happening here." Wynter smiled, watching her wife play with the children.

"But you are bringing attention to the children, and this is so good."

"What you are doing is good," Wynter told her. "You are giving these children lives."

Marie nodded sadly. "We are trying."

As they walked around, Marie would tell Wynter about the children. "This little girl, she lost her mother; her father is alive, but he had to go far away to find work, so she stays here with us." The little girl looked up at Wynter, giving her a toothy grin. Wynter smiled back at her.

They walked to another room and encountered a little girl sitting by herself on a window ledge. The girl was looking out at the planting beds in the garden. Marie walked Wynter over to the window.

"This is Roseline, she likes to watch the plants grow." Marie smiled at the little girl. "Here we plant vegetables; we teach the children how to do this, and it feeds them too."

Roseline was small, and had her hair pulled back into two lobsided ponytails.

"Bonjou, Roseline," Wynter said to the child.

Roseline looked up at Wynter, her eyes dark pools of sadness. "Bonjou," she replied very quietly, then she turned to look back at the vegetable beds, her hands folded in her lap.

As they walked away, Wynter glanced back, curious if the child would watch them go, but she didn't.

"What's her story?" Wynter asked.

"Oh," Marie shook her head, "Roseline and her brother, Samuel, lost both their parents in the earthquake. It took two days to unbury them." Marie winced. "They'd been sitting by their dead mother all that time."

"Oh my God," Wynter breathed. "That's so awful."

Marie nodded. "Samuel is doing better, but little Roseline seems to shrink a little more each day."

"Bonjou," Remi said to the little boy coloring a picture at one of the desks. "Kisa wap desen?" She asked him what he was drawing.

"Yon tank," the boy answered, smiling up at Remi. His dark eyes widened as he looked at her. "Ou se Remington La Roché!" he exclaimed, recognizing her.

"Wi." Remi nodded. "Epi ou ye?" She asked his name.

"Mwen se Samuel. Ou se di!" he exclaimed, telling her that she was tough.

Remington laughed, nodding to the boy.

Wynter found Remi a half an hour later, playing trucks with Samuel.

"Samuel, sa a se Wynter madanm mwen." Remi introduced Wynter as her wife.

"Madanm mwen?" Samuel queried, surprised by the title.

"Wi, madanm mwen," Remi confirmed.

"Petit ou gen chans." Samuel smiled, saying that her child was lucky.

"Poukisa gen chans?" Remi asked why.

"De manmans!" Samuel qualified, saying two moms.

Remington laughed, nodding her head. "He said our child is lucky because the child would have two moms."

Wynter chuckled. "He's not wrong." Her eyes sparkled. "Did you say his name is Samuel?"

"Yes, why?"

"Because I just met his sister, Roseline. Both of their parents were killed in the quake last year," she said, smiling down at Samuel, who was now staring up at her with a bright smile.

She looked at Remi and canted her head. "I'm having a thought…"

You can find more information about the author and other books in the *WeHo* series here:

www.sherrylhancock.com

www.facebook.com/SherrylDHancock

www.vulpine-press.com/we-ho

Also by Sherryl D. Hancock:

The *MidKnight Blue* series. Dive into the world of Midnight Chevalier and as we follow her transformation from gang leader to cop from the very beginning.

www.vulpine-press.com/midknight-blue-series

The *Wild Irish Silence* series. Escape into the world of BJ Sparks and discover how he went from the small-town boy to the world-famous rock star.

www.vulpine-press.com/wild-irish-silence-series